# *The* PRACTICE
## *of* PERFECTION

# *The* PRACTICE
# *of* PERFECTION

*Mary Frances* COADY

COTEAU BOOKS

© Mary Frances Coady, 2009

All rights reserved. No part of this publication may be reproduced, stored in a retrieval system or transmitted, in any form or by any means, without the prior written consent of the publisher or a licence from The Canadian Copyright Licensing Agency (Access Copyright). For an Access Copyright licence, visit www.accesscopyright.ca or call toll free to 1-800-893-5777.

These stories are works of fiction. Names, characters, places, and incidents either are the product of the author's imagination or are used fictitiously. Any resemblance to actual persons, living or dead, is coincidental.

Edited by Edna Alford
Cover and series design by Duncan Campbell
Cover photo: Kamil Vojnar, Photonica Collection/Getty Images

Printed and bound in Canada at Friesens
This book is printed on FSC-certified paper

**Library and Archives Canada Cataloguing in Publication**

Coady, Mary Frances
The practice of perfection / Mary Frances Coady.

ISBN 978-1-55050-400-2

1. Convents--Fiction. I. Title

PS8555.O232 P73 2009     C813'.54     C2009-901008-9

10 9 8 7 6 5 4 3 2 1

Mixed Sources
Cert no. SW-COC-001271
© 1996 FSC

COTEAU BOOKS
2517 Victoria Avenue
Regina, Saskatchewan
Canada   S4P 0T2

AVAILABLE IN CANADA FROM:
Publishers Group Canada
9050 Shaughnessy Street
Vancouver, BC, Canada   V6P 6E5

The publisher gratefully acknowledges the financial assistance of the Saskatchewan Arts Board, the Canada Council for the Arts, the Government of Canada through the Book Publishing Industry Development Program (BPIDP), Association for the Export of Canadian Books, and the City of Regina Arts Commission, for its publishing program.

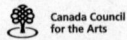

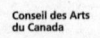

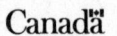

*For Maria Ertis*

CONTENTS

All that is in the World – 1

Practice of Perfection – 23

Feast of the Purification – 43

Composition of Place – 65

Silence Pages – 83

Mother and All Her Chicks – 107

Particular Friendship – 129

Angels of their Own – 159

O Come Emmanuel – 177

Holy Innocents – 193

## *All that is in the World*

"IN THE WINTER THE RIVER NEVER FREEZES completely; it's always flowing underneath," said Mother Alphonsine. "The ice is deceptive."

The nun stood at the edge of the riverbank looking down at the mounds of ice covering the narrow river. She held a black shawl tightly around her head and shoulders, clasping it at her chest with a sharply veined hand.

Clustered around her, staring down at the white expanse, stood four postulants, each wearing a long black dress and a cape that was topped with a Peter Pan collar. Each wore a black woolen shawl like Mother Alphonsine's around her shoulders. Overhead, the branches of a giant weeping willow, heavy with the weight of newly fallen snow, drooped low over the group.

"When it breaks there, in the centre . . ." the nun took her hand from where it had clutched her shawl and pointed out toward the river, her arm suspended in mid-air, "... down in there, when you can actually see the water flowing again, then, *then,* you know spring is here." She looked around at them, her eyes smiling behind round wire-rimmed glasses. "In the meantime, we live in hope." She looked around the circle again. "Shall we move on?"

She turned, clasped her shawl tighter and made her way back through the snow to the path. The postulants shifted and turned in ragtag fashion, stamping the snow from the rubber boots that fit snugly over their new black lace-up shoes, and fell in step around her when they reached the shovelled area.

The four of them had been in the novitiate less than twenty-four hours, having been admitted the day before, the feast of the Epiphany, six days into the new year of 1959. Melanie and Annette had arrived together. From the car, Melanie had seen Annette walking along the bridge carrying a suitcase, a pale blue angora scarf wrapped around her neck. When the car reached the convent gate, Melanie retrieved her cello from the front seat. Her father opened the trunk and took out her suitcase, and was about to carry it up the steps when she stopped him and, with a hurried kiss and a wave to her brothers in the back seat, took the case from him, opened the gate and walked slowly toward the front door. There she waited for Annette, and together the two girls rang the doorbell.

The door opened immediately and Mother Alphonsine, the novice mistress, stood there, all smiles. "Welcome to the last of our new postulants!" she said, kissing each of them on both cheeks. "Here you are, like the Magi, answering the call. Following the star. The two others are already here." Another nun took Melanie's cello, and Mother Alphonsine ushered the two of them through the green-curtained doorway of the cloister into a bare room where the other two postulants were struggling with unfamiliar black clothes. Their own clothes, the ones they were leaving behind, lay in scattered, colourful heaps on the floor. The novice mistress introduced the two newcomers, saying with a broad smile, "You're strangers to each other now, but soon you'll be fast friends."

THEY NOW MOVED ALONG the newly shovelled path in jerky steps, still in a cluster around Mother Alphonsine. She led the way along the chapel side of the convent. "When it snows there's good exercise in running a shovel along the walkways," she said. She glanced backwards and her eyes settled on a chubby postulant with dark, wary eyes, who had been introduced as Carol. "Have you shovelled snow before, Carol?" She had a slightly teasing smile.

Carol reddened. "Not much, Mother."

"Well, there's lots of opportunity here," the nun went on. "Not to mention weeding the garden in the summer and raking the leaves in the fall and washing windows in the spring." She looked around the group, still smiling. "That's all I'll say about work for the moment. After all, this is only your first day, and we have to ease you in gently."

They rounded the back end of the chapel and came upon an expanse of lawn. "There's the Grotto of Our Lady," she said, indicating a shrine at one end. It was made of rocks, and a statue was set in on a ledge. "And behind there," she added, indicating a hedge to the left, "is the garden."

"That's a big garden, Mother. Do we have to look after it?" asked the fourth postulant, named Edith, whose pale face was flecked with freckles and whose hair, even beneath the black net, shone a brilliant red-blonde. She smiled as she spoke.

Mother Alphonsine looked at Edith with a gaze that was half quizzical, half smiling. "Do you mean, 'May we look after the garden,' Edith? Here, we always look for opportunities to be generous." She paused. "Two of the nuns have charge of the garden, but as I have said, the novices and postulants are most useful as weed pullers." Edith's smile remained stiffly in place. The group, more scattered now, moved in silence onto the path that crossed the lawn. Annette lagged behind, scraping the pink pearl nail polish from her fingers with the edge of her thumbnail. Melanie turned and waited for her.

"Did you ask her about your cello?" whispered Annette.

Melanie shook her head and put her finger to her lips.

"I'm ready for a nap." Annette dropped her head to one side and closed her eyes, simulating sleep. Then she grinned, revealing uneven teeth and a dimple low in her right cheek.

The five-thirty wake-up bell had sounded like a fire alarm in the corridor outside the large dormitory, where they slept in assigned beds surrounded by white cotton curtains. Bodies thudded to the floor, and some moments later the postulants stomped down the back staircase one behind another, bleary eyed, emerging at the chapel door. Mother Alphonsine ushered them to the pews in front of the novices. The chapel was in semi-darkness. The red sanctuary lamp hung in its gold casing before the tabernacle. On the side altar straight ahead, in front of the statue of Our Lady, light from a votive candle danced against a brass pot of yellow chrysanthemums. The occasional cough and rustle of skirts and rosary beads broke the cold early morning silence.

The group had by now reached the tall hedge that separated the convent grounds from the buildings beyond. Behind them, a bell sounded inside the convent.

"Oh, my goodness," said Mother Alphonsine, reaching under her shawl and pulling out a watch that hung from a black strap. "It's time for the examen." She turned abruptly and began to walk back toward the building. Again, the postulants shifted and followed her.

She spoke more quickly now. "The examen is that time of the day – there are two times, actually: now, just before noon, and at the end of the day after night prayers – it's the two times when we look at how we have spent this day so far. We examine our actions, our thoughts, our motivations. It's a time to reflect on whether or not we have been pleasing to God. This is when we render an account to Him."

She strode toward the door by the side of the chapel, increasing speed. The postulants tried to hurry behind her, awkward in their bulky clothes. Annette stumbled on her skirt. She looked at Melanie and grinned, the dimple on her cheek deepening.

The two had been school friends for almost two years, ever since Annette had caught up with Melanie on the street after an afternoon concert on the Feast of St. Monica, the school's patron. Melanie had played her cello at the concert; a solo piece called "Humoresque" and, accompanied by another girl on the piano, "The Skye Boat Song."

"What is that big violin thing?" Annette called, hurrying up behind her.

Melanie stopped and set the cello case on the sidewalk while she adjusted the books she was carrying in her other arm. "A cello."

"I've never heard of it before. It was real nice what you played. It sounded like someone singing. Singing without words."

"Well, thanks. I've only been playing a couple of years. My father thought a cello would be good for me to play. He plays the violin, and I guess he thought that with my two brothers playing the violin and the viola, we'd make a string quartet. It didn't work out that way, because my brothers aren't even remotely interested in playing an instrument. All they want to play is football." She laughed. "But I like the cello. Even though it's hard on my arm." She moved her right arm back and forth, her face in a grimace.

"But —" Annette gave Melanie a sly sideways glance. "Nobody ever told you it was unladylike having your legs like that while you're playing? I mean, putting your legs around the cello?"

Melanie gave a small laugh, her face blushing. "Well, playing it with the uniform on did seem kind of strange." She looked down and moved her feet apart until her legs stretched her burgundy uniform skirt to its full width. "I usually play it with a wider skirt on, so it's not so bad." Still blushing, she reached back and twisted her dark ponytail.

Annette deepened her voice and lowered her chin until it almost touched her chest. "A girl from St. Monica's! Spreading her legs! I'm shocked!"

They both laughed, Melanie pink faced with embarrassment. She picked up her cello in its case and together the pair went off to Connie's Coffee Shop, the favourite after-school haunt of St. Monica's students. This excursion became a daily routine; as many girls as possible squeezed into one of the booths, joined by two or three boys from St. Paul's Boys' School, and ordered Cokes and milkshakes. On Friday evenings, a group of them often crowded into a car belonging to one of the girls and drove to the drive-in theatre.

One day, as the two of them were walking home along the sidewalk, where the high brick wall enclosed the convent grounds adjacent to the school,

Melanie confided to Annette that, in confession, a priest had asked her if she ever considered entering a religious order.

"Did you tell him where to go?" said Annette.

"Well, I was kind of surprised, but then I started thinking about it."

"Wha-a-t?!" Annette stopped and stared at her friend.

"Well, I am."

"Are you crazy? How can you lock yourself up like that?"

"First of all, you don't get locked up. Does Sister Zelie look like she's locked up? Or Sister Donalda? You know these nuns better than I do. You had them ever since you started kindergarten. I've only had them at St. Monica's."

"Yeah, I really liked Sister Ruth Ann. But anyway, what about your cello?"

"I might still be able to play it. But if I can't, the bigger the sacrifice you make, the more grace you get. That's what the priest said. What good does it do to give your whole life if you're going to hold something back?" She tossed back her ponytail. "Anyway, I said I'm only *thinking* about it. There's nothing wrong with *thinking*, is there?"

They reached the back gate of the convent. "Let's see if there are any novices there," said Annette. Her dimple flashed. "If you look through the crack between the gate and the wall, you can sometimes see them." She ran over and peered inside. "Nope."

They dropped the topic until several weeks later,

when St. Monica's held its annual students' retreat day. A young priest stood alone on the stage of the auditorium as the classes filed in and took their seats. He had dark wavy hair and wore a white robe with a hood at the back and a flowing black cape. One of the nuns said he was a Dominican.

"He looks like a pelican," whispered Annette to Melanie as they came in the door.

"Or a magpie or a penguin," said another girl nearby.

The school principal, Sister Beatrice, introduced the priest as Father Raymond. He strode back and forth across the stage, taking long steps in heavy black shoes, his black cape swishing around his white robe every time he turned. "It's my guess," he said, "that perhaps ten of you in front of me, give or take a couple, have a vocation to the religious life." He shaded his eyes with his hands and pretended to peer out at the assembly and then resumed walking back and forth. "Oh, I know you may not like the idea of becoming nuns, and you might find yourselves fighting the very idea of it, but you must listen to God's quiet voice. Because if God is calling you to the religious life, there is nothing you will be able to do to get away from that call. I know. I did everything I could to avoid entering religious life, but it all came up empty for me. So finally I said, 'All right, God, you win.' And do you know what? From that day on, I've felt such peace, felt such joy."

There was not a sound throughout the assembly. The nuns who were standing in the side aisles had tiptoed to available chairs. "Now I just want you to picture yourself for a moment," he continued, "in a nun's habit, sailing away on a boat, perhaps toward Africa or the Far East. You're leaving all that's familiar to you – your language, your climate, your family and your sisters in community. You're off to learn a new language, to adjust to a new climate, to meet new people, people who are not even Christian. And –" he paused and looked around, "you are going to a leper colony. 'I wouldn't do that for a million dollars,' says someone. And what do you reply?" He stopped suddenly, his cape swirling around him, and looked back and forth across his audience. "You answer, 'Neither would I.' Because you are giving your life in this way for a spiritual reward that is far, far greater than any material reward." He folded his arms and strode back and forth, staring down at the stage floor.

"Or again," he said, stopping in mid-stride and once again facing his audience, "picture yourself going into an enclosed monastery, cut off from the world. Perhaps you never see your family again, and if you do it's through a monastic grille. You get up at four o'clock every morning and you spend six or seven hours a day in prayer, but this is not self-punishment." He paused, his eyes intent on the assembly, as if searching for someone. "It's a sacrifice that you carry out for a greater good – to win souls and to make up for all the sin in the world. Or again: teaching or nursing here at home, pouring your life out. Why do it? To escape from the world? No, and if you do, it will soon be found out, because the life will prove too difficult for you. But what a glorious thing it is, not just to be married to one man and be mother to a few children, but to be married to Our Lord Himself, and to be a spiritual mother to the whole world. It is the most sublime calling a girl can hope for. And the small sacrifices that are demanded are minuscule compared with the rewards that she reaps for herself and for others. And so, are there some generous souls out there among you?" Again he shaded his eyes and bent forward, scanning the assembly.

Melanie and Annette looked at each other, both expressionless.

At the end of the retreat day they rang the front doorbell of the convent and asked to speak to Mother Alphonsine, who insisted that she speak to them separately. To each of them she gave the same response: "If you're sure that God is calling you to this life, continue to pray about it and then enter soon. Do not delay in answering God's call." To Melanie she added, "What a wonderful gift it is to offer your musical talent to God. Your cello may be used to give praise, or perhaps you may be asked to make the sacrifice. It's all in God's good time." And to Annette: "God often chooses high-spirited, fun-loving girls like you to serve Him alone. And you will give all of yourself generously, I'm sure of it."

"These girls' retreats," said a St. Paul's boy, half hanging out of the booth at Connie's Coffee Shop. He sucked at the bottom of a milkshake glass through a straw. "It always takes you at least a month to get away from the idea of being a nun."

But the idea had become a prospect, and then a reality. "It's kind of exciting to give up everything, isn't it?" said Melanie one day.

Annette nodded. "I guess so. I haven't really thought about it that way. But my mother's sure thrilled. She goes around saying, 'My daughter's going to be a nun!' As if I'm going to be canonized a saint or something. That'll be the day. But yeah, it's kind of a good feeling."

ON THEIR SECOND DAY, the postulants were introduced to their cleaning charges. A novice by the name of Sister Louise, her white veil tied back, handed Melanie a blue apron. "This is for your use," she said in a soft voice. "Mother said you can embroider your initials on the top at recreation today." Melanie fitted the apron over her head. Sister Louise held a mop and handed Melanie a feather duster, and the two headed down the corridor and into the novices' common room.

This was the room the four postulants had been brought to the first evening. They had trailed behind Mother Alphonsine as she led them through the door. Twelve novices sat on straight-backed chairs around a long table covered with brown oilcloth. The novices had shifted their black-draped bodies toward the door, their beaming faces framed with white veils and wimples. They giggled and exclaimed as the postulants shuffled into the room, some of them half standing to get a better look at the new arrivals.

The room was empty now, the walls on either side of the long table lined with school desks. Each postulant had been allotted a desk where she was to keep her missal and her copies of the New Testament and *The Imitation of Christ*. Brown cupboards were set in against the back wall. Melanie looked out the window at the weeping willow, still laden with snow, and at the chunks of ice clinging to the riverbank.

"Our work is a meditation," Mother Alphonsine had said earlier, before the group had dispersed to do their charges. "We offer it to God with all our hearts. We try to be recollected at all times, to remember the fruits of our morning's meditation, not to let our thoughts go helter-skelter, especially not to let our thoughts go back to the world we have left behind." She held up a copy of *The Imitation of Christ* in one hand, the thumb of the other hand inserted between the pages. "'All that is in the world is vanity except to love God and to serve Him only,'" she read. "Do everything for the glory of God and the salvation of souls," she said, closing the book. "You dust out a corner thoroughly, you peel a potato with care; these are small actions that are like pearls in God's sight when you offer them up with love. They are not done to make us holy, but if we let Him – if we remain faithful to the duty of the moment – God Himself will make us holy."

Melanie shifted from her knees to her feet, and, gathering her skirt about her legs, waddled squat-legged from desk to desk, reaching back to the baseboards. "They'll get you using some elbow grease in there, wait and see," her father had said shortly before she left home. "You won't be reading magazines." His voice had a half-teasing and half-warning tone.

"Uh-uh, Dad," she replied, "we'll be learning things like Latin and philosophy and theology. And we'll be reading spiritual books."

She stopped and blinked her eyes hard, reaching in her pocket for the large white handkerchief she had been given on the first day.

"Melanie is a musician," said Mother Alphonsine at afternoon recreation. The postulants had quickly learned that two hours in the day – one in the afternoon and the other in the early evening – were set aside for recreation. The rest of the day was spent in almost total silence. The first evening they had been ushered into the tiny refectory in the basement, where they had been given their places at a narrow horseshoe-shaped table. Everyone ate facing downwards, the scraping of plates and clinking of cutlery the only sounds.

Now, for recreation, they sat with the novices in a semicircle facing the novice mistress, every black lap covered with a flowered cloth, on which each one had some mending or crochet or embroidery. No one spoke to each other, but addressed only the novice mistress. "We safeguard against lack of charity and idle chatter when we refrain from speaking to each other," Mother Alphonsine had explained.

"Melanie plays the cello," she continued now, looking around the group. Laughter and exclamations erupted. "The cello!" said one novice over by the window. "Is that like a banjo, Mother?" asked another.

"No, Mother, it's like a violin, only bigger." Melanie looked over at Annette.

Annette's shoulders were shaking. She burst out in a spray of laughter. "It's a joke, Mother," she said. "The cello, I mean. I used to tease Melanie about it."

"What was the joke?" asked Mother Alphonsine.

Annette reddened and she looked at Melanie, her cheeks puffed as if suppressing an explosion of giggles. Melanie looked down at the untouched needlework in her lap. Neither spoke.

Finally, Annette swallowed and straightened her face. "It's nothing really, Mother."

"But surely if there's something funny, you can share the joke with us, Annette. Is the cello such a funny instrument?"

"The way it's played it is," said Annette, adding in a whisper, "between the knees." She burst once again into giggles.

Mother Alphonsine's lips tightened. "Perhaps you can tell us about the cello, Melanie."

"Well, I don't know, Mother," began Melanie. "My music teacher said that the cello is closer than any other instrument to the sound of the human voice. So when you play the cello it's almost like singing."

"Seriously, Mother, Melanie plays it really well," said Annette. "She used to play at all the school concerts, sometimes alone and sometimes with the piano." The dimple deepened in her cheek and she looked ready to break into laughter again. "I mean it."

She looked over at Melanie, her face now serious. "It was beautiful."

"Actually, it's better than singing, Mother," said Melanie. "Because when you're playing you feel as if you're surrounded by music on all sides."

"It must be hard to lug around, Mother," said one of the novices.

"No, not really," said Melanie. "It goes in a case with a handle and you carry it like that." She made a fist with her right hand and crooked her arm to demonstrate. "You have to be careful when you put it in the car, though. You prop it up in the front seat, and so it rides along just like a person."

Mother Alphonsine laughed. "I don't think we'll be taking it with us in a car any time soon. Unless it goes back home. At any rate, I don't see that there will be time for practicing the cello now, although who knows in the future. For now, I think not. A piano might be different. If any of you plays the piano, there might be some use for that. Piano skills can always be transferred to the organ. But any other instrument . . ." her voice trailed off. "A novice brought her accordion a few years ago, and it was returned with dispatch."

Annette looked over at Melanie. Melanie's needlework remained in her lap, still untouched.

"THE POSTULANTS will wash their hair this afternoon," Mother Alphonsine announced after her morning conference two days later. From around the brown common-room table the postulants turned to face her. "You wash your hair once a week in the washroom sinks across from the dormitory. You can take off your capes and dresses and hang them on the hooks in the washroom." She paused and smiled. "You are used to hair dryers and such things in the world. You will notice that here we don't have them. Towel dry your hair well, and let nature do the rest."

The postulants trailed across the hall from the dormitory to the washroom and began to strip down to their white long-sleeved undervests and grey petticoats in front of the row of sinks.

Suddenly Annette let out a whoop. "Girls, we're alone. We can talk!"

Edith looked at her. "I don't think we should be talking. We're supposed to be keeping silence." She reached up and pulled the black net from her head. Red-blonde hair streamed down around her shoulders.

"You're right," said Melanie, looking around. "Mother Alphonsine probably doesn't want us to be alone together. She'll think we're comparing notes."

"Well, *let's* compare notes!" said Annette, laughing as she pulled her dress over her head. Her laugh had a muffled sound against the serge material. "I'll never get used to putting these clothes on, there's so many of them!"

"How do you like it so far?" asked Carol from the sink next to Melanie's. "Are you glad you came?"

"I think so," said Melanie, raising her voice above the running water as she lathered her hair. "Actually,

I like the silence. You don't use up your thoughts on a lot of silly talk. But I get tired of being regulated every minute. And the rules. Having to get permission for everything. I don't see the point. Do you?"

Carol stood still, her head poised above the sink. "If you're going to start questioning every little thing, you might as well give up right now. That's what I think, anyway." She began massaging her head with quick strokes, large gobs of shampoo froth clinging to her hands.

"It's nice to be by ourselves for a while, even just once," said Edith. She rubbed her head with one hand and held onto a small shampoo bottle with the other. "But wouldn't you like just to go out for a hamburger and a milkshake? Just once?"

"I'm shocked, Sister," said Annette, speaking into the sink with mock surprise, her voice hollow. "Such secular thoughts!"

Melanie unplugged her sink to let out the soapy water. "I guess the idea is that you strip away everything so that you're left with the one thing necessary, like Jesus says in the Gospel."

Edith turned her face toward Melanie. One eye remained closed as the water continued to rush over the side of her head. "It's really simple when you think about it that way. You give up everything and give your life to God," she said. "That's the only reason why anybody's here, I guess."

"But can't you give your life to God without having all these rules hanging over your head?" Melanie looked down the row of sinks toward Edith.

Edith stood straight, her shining limp hair piled upon her head. "We probably need them to get the secular life out of our systems. That's what it is to be a nun. You have to follow a lot of rules. If you want to live a life of perfection, you have to learn how to do it, and that's what Mother Alphonsine is trying to teach us."

Annette looked over at Melanie, her eyes half hidden by wet strands of hair. "I still don't know why you can't play your cello."

"Well, I wasn't very good at it anyway."

"You were so! They didn't have the right to take it away from you."

"Maybe I can still play it. Mother Alphonsine hasn't sent it home."

Annette reached for her towel. "Just wait."

The water was no longer running from the taps, and a sudden stillness filled the room. The postulants caught their hair up in towels, turban-style. Annette looked at her face in the small mirror on the wall. "Who's the scarecrow?" she said, and then moved over to the window and plopped down on the broad sill. She hoisted up her petticoat, spread her black-stockinged legs and leaned back against the window.

"What are you doing?" asked Melanie.

"I'm seeing what it would be like for you to play the cello with a habit on. I think it'll be pretty easy." She bent over and moved her right arm back and forth along the strings of an imaginary instrument. She began to hum tunelessly in a low tone. Melanie laughed. "You're crazy."

The other two began to giggle. Annette continued, her movements becoming more exaggerated, her left hand now near her shoulder, the fingers curved and shaking as if pressing on the instrument's strings. Her right hand cut back and forth across her body, her hum sliding into a low chant. Her eyes were closed now, her body swaying back and forth.

The other three stopped laughing and began to sway in rhythm with her. Annette's right arm cut a wider and wider arc and her head rolled down and then back, her eyes still closed, her chant an incantation. The towel had fallen onto her shoulders, and her hair fell in limp strands. The other postulants began to hum with her and then, one by one, they opened their mouths in wordless chant. Their bodies swayed and their voices rose and fell in a blend beyond unison and harmony. They moved and swayed in their white vests and grey petticoats, their towel-turbans loosening and falling down around them as they faced Annette, her wild right arm surging back and forth with her imaginary bow, her left shaking and pressing on make-believe strings. The chant grew louder and stronger until it filled the small washroom and then even seemed to reach beyond the walls.

The door opened and one of the novices stood in the doorway, fingering the black rosary that hung from her waist. There was a frown on her face.

The chanting ceased. Annette opened her eyes and stood up straight, her petticoat falling around her legs. Her mouth hung open for a second, then closed over her uneven teeth. Edith reached for her dress from its hook, her cheeks ablaze. The novice watched as, in silence, the postulants dressed themselves and arranged the nets on their hair. Melanie and Annette, pulling their dresses on, faced the window. Outside, the snow-covered expanse of lawn stretched down to the river and, past the weeping willow, across to the brick wall.

# *Practice of Perfection*

"'There lived a woman named Bona who was as good as her name suggested. She suffered a most severe infirmity in her breasts, which were so eaten away by cancer and so full of worms that it would have been an insufferable torment for any other person. Bona, however, suffered it with patience and thanksgiving.'"

Sister Lucy paused, straightened and pressed the fingertips of her left hand along her left temple, shifting the starched white band that stretched across her forehead. She then lowered her head, continuing to read aloud.

"'St. Dominic loved her much because of her suffering and her advanced virtue. One day, having confessed and communicated her, he asked to see her terrible wound. When Bona uncovered herself and the saint saw the putrid mass of the cancer swarming with worms, he was moved to compassion and begged her to give him one of the worms as a relic.'"

A noise sounding like a stifled gasp broke in at Sister Lucy's immediate left. From the corner of her eye she saw that the white veil of the novice sitting next to her was shaking. The novice, Sister Camillus, held a small piece of white linen in one hand and a needle attached to a string of brilliant red embroidery thread in the other. Her body was hunched over the needlework as if in a state of spasm. Sister Lucy again pressed her fingers against her forehead, then shifted the large book against the edge of the table and resumed reading.

"'*Bona told him she would not allow him to take a worm from her breast unless he promised to return it; for she had come to such a pitch of joy in seeing herself thus devoured alive that whenever one of the worms fell to the ground, she picked it up and restored it to its place. So on his word of honour she gave St. Dominic a worm that was well grown and had a black head.*'"

Sister Camillus had by now lowered her needlework to her lap. Her head was bent into her chest, and her whole body was so convulsed with laughter that Sister Lucy could hear the rattle of the rosary beads hanging from the belt at her waist. Sister Lucy looked down the length of the plain brown table. On either side, facing each other, their backs erect and their white-veiled heads bent over their needlework, sat the eleven other novices, and behind them, the four recently arrived postulants. All seemed composed and serene.

Sister Lucy continued: "'*Immediately the worm turned into a most beautiful pearl. As St. Dominic was handing it back to the woman, it became a worm again, and she put it in her breasts, where it had been bred.'"*

Sister Camillus's suppressed laughter now began to sound like the faint cries of a wild beast. Sister Lucy looked up at Mother Alphonsine, the novice mistress, who sat at the head of the table, directly facing her. Her head, draped in the black veil of the professed nun, was bent over the billowing folds of the altar cloth she was embroidering, her eyes riveted as if in total concentration. The nun's round, wire-rimmed glasses sat halfway down her nose. Her lips were slightly pursed. For a brief second Sister Lucy wondered if she too was tempted to break out into uncontrollable laughter.

On the wall behind Mother Alphonsine hung a large picture of the Sacred Heart. This was a close-up of Jesus, His gaze fixed so far upward that only the whites of His eyes showed. Halfway down the picture the index finger of His right hand pointed to His exposed heart, which radiated with yellow streams. Encircling it was a crown of thorns from which fell three drops of blood. The heart itself was pink and fleshy.

Sister Lucy pulled her gaze back to the book, shifted slightly in her chair, straightened, and continued reading. "*'As St. Dominic was leaving, Bona's cancer-eaten breasts fell off from her, worms and all; and the flesh began to grow –'*"

An electric bell sounded in the hall outside the novices' common room. "This ends today's reading, 'On Conformity to the Will of God' from *Practice of Perfection and Christian Virtue*," Sister Lucy intoned.

"Praise be to Jesus," said Mother Alphonsine, folding up the altar cloth. There was a catch in her voice, and her face twitched before settling into an expression of recollected calm.

"Amen," Sister Lucy responded, closing the book and making the sign of the cross.

Around her, in a silent flurry, the novices packed their sewing into small black bags and rose from their chairs for their visit to chapel. Sister Camillus remained seated, her body looking like a limp rag doll. She turned toward Sister Lucy. Her eyes were watery and red-rimmed, her whole face caught in a look of helpless laughter.

"It h-had a b-black h-head!" she whispered, her voice shaking, the words exploding from her lips in a shower of tiny bubbles. Her body twisted itself once again into a spasmodic convulsion. Sister Lucy looked away, ran the tips of her fingers along her left eyebrow, then got up stiffly from her chair and headed toward the door.

Downstairs, the whole community was converging on the chapel for the evening visit to the Blessed Sacrament, the thirty or so nuns and the twelve novices and four postulants who were in training to make their vows of poverty, chastity and obedience. By the time the clock on the back wall struck six, each one was in her place, kneeling in silent adoration before the tabernacle which sat in the middle of the altar. Locked inside the tabernacle was the Blessed Sacrament.

The nuns and novices all wore the same habit, a long shapeless black dress tied at the waist with a leather belt from which dangled a large rosary with brown beads. On each head was a veil, black or white depending on each one's vowed status, that covered the shoulders and fell to the waist.

Sister Lucy stared at the green curtain hanging in front of the tabernacle door, and then at the gilded lettering etched in the white high altar: "Jesus My Lord My God My All." Hands clasped tightly, she tried forming words in her mind. "Oh God, oh God," she began. Nothing more came. Around her, she heard sounds of rosary beads against pews, soft breathing, quiet coughs. From behind came sniffling and a quick, muffled snort into a handkerchief. Sister Camillus probably. The after-effects of her giggling fit. "Oh God, oh Jesus," she began again. Her mind was dry, blank. She reached into her pocket for her own handkerchief. She didn't need it, but the action gave her something to do. It also made her head tilt a bit, a movement that gave some relief to the stiffness that was beginning to develop in her neck.

The pockets were the feature she liked best about the cumbersome habit. In fact, they weren't part of the habit at all; they were cloth saddlebags that hung from a waistband. Slits along the sides of the habit skirt allowed access to them. Inside one of Sister Lucy's pockets were her large white handkerchief, a pen and a black sheath that contained a small pair of scissors.

Inside the other pocket was her permissions book, a small booklet made of pages sewn from used envelopes, in which a novice recorded the virtues she was striving to attain and the penances she was currently performing. Within the same pocket was a small string contraption formed from a complicated set of knots and made to resemble a horsewhip. This was called a discipline. The novice was to use the discipline to whip herself once a month in one of the small rooms at the end of the novitiate corridor. Mother Alphonsine had explained its use to the novices. "Men religious use the discipline on their backs and women religious use it –" she had hesitated briefly – "where they sit down."

To Sister Lucy, the discipline seemed a pathetic remnant of hair shirts and chains. She had gone once to one of the rooms, had taken the limp little thing in her hands and had pulled up the voluminous skirts of her habit and blue petticoat. She had pulled down her oversized underpants. It seemed strange and incongruous to be gazing down at the white of her thigh and the taut elastic garter holding up her black stocking. She stood by the window and, holding on to her volume of skirts, gave a half-hearted swat. She looked out at the expanse of lawn where the handyman was pushing the lawnmower. She thought of the whole court of heaven watching her – God the Father on His throne; Jesus; the Holy Ghost; the Blessed Virgin Mary, the Queen of Heaven herself with her retinue of baby angels and wavy-haired virgin martyrs holding palm branches; St. Ignatius and St. Francis Xavier and all the other great saints of the Church who had gone about with fire in their eyes and the cross of Jesus Christ in their hands. These men had been the backbone of the faith down through the ages. She thought of St. Theresa, the Little Flower of Jesus, holding a sensuous splash of roses against her brown Carmelite robe, her pink lips curled into a kewpie-doll smile. Sister Lucy thought of the whole kingdom of heaven crowded into the little room to watch her, and she felt overcome with shame and embarrassment. She quickly hoisted up her underpants, adjusted her skirt and left the room. She had never returned.

Sister Lucy joined her hands again, slowly intertwining her fingers. She felt a twinge between her left shoulder and her neck and slumped back from where she was kneeling, then inched her way onto the seat of the pew, trying to look inconspicuous. She looked up at the altar and the green curtain at its centre, but could think of nothing but the line of pain that reached up through her neck into her left temple. Her neck had been wrenched a couple of years earlier when she'd fallen off her bicycle on the steep hill just behind her family's farmhouse. The hill had always been daunting to her, but she had given it a try in a moment of daring. Halfway down she panicked and lost control. Her legs shot straight ahead and she leaned back, trying in vain to stop. The bicycle rolled over on top of her. When she picked herself up, pain shot up through her head. It never amounted to anything, however, never hurt enough for her to see a doctor. The bruises on her arms and the cuts on her hands healed quickly enough, but from time to time her neck still gave a twinge and the left side of her head throbbed with a dull ache. Sister Lucy wasn't quite sure if it was pain or not. It was perhaps only discomfort.

Her mind went back to the reading in the common room. She could understand Sister Camillus's fit of the giggles. *Practice of Perfection and Christian Virtue* was a book on virtues that people in religious life were meant to practise. Each treatise ended with a chapter called, "What has been said is now confirmed by examples." These chapters were Sister Lucy's personal favourites, because they gave far-fetched examples of medieval monks and crazy people living in the desert. The examples, like the priest who had an inordinate attachment to his mother and was dogged at every step by the devil mocking him with cries of "Mummy, Mummy," often reduced the novices to ridicule and laughter at recreation.

An early evening gloom had come upon the chapel. The red flicker of the sanctuary lamp sent shadows against the white backdrop of the high altar. Sister Lucy thought about the innocent and radiant Bona, the woman who had let her breasts be eaten alive. Had God really wanted her to suffer like that? Was this what it meant to be holy? She looked over at the side altar of the Blessed Virgin Mary, which stood near the wall to the left of the high altar. The head of the statue faced downwards, the arms extended on either side, the hands open. The folds of her tunic fell down over a flat chest and shapeless body. Had worms eaten up *her* breasts too? Sister Lucy looked quickly back at the high altar, shocked at the flippant thought.

Suddenly feeling tired, she closed her eyes and saw herself as Bona, walking about serene and beautiful, a long white shift hugging her body, golden hair streaming down her back. Underneath, her breasts were wasting away, worms crawling in and out, eating the flesh. Occasionally a look of pain crossed her face; otherwise she let no one know of the ravages within. It was a secret between herself and God. Then the sensitive St. Dominic came upon her and praised God for her holy suffering.

She opened her eyes and shifted her body. Should she tell Mother Alphonsine about the throbbing in her left temple? Would this be the holy thing to do? Maybe the novice mistress would tell her she was being soft on herself. "A little sacrifice is necessary for all of us, my dear Sister," she might say. Was this why Bona didn't go to a doctor, why she refused to wash out the putrid mass of poison from her breasts? Did she believe that God was demanding this sacrifice from her?

Their half-hour visit to chapel was now over, and the novices filed downstairs to the refectory for supper. Sister Lucy noticed that by this time Sister Camillus had composed herself and, like the others, walked straight and erect with head slightly bowed. The refectory was a tiny cell of a room with a table shaped like a horseshoe. At the head of the table a single chair indicated the novice mistress's place. Pushed underneath the two sides were fourteen stools.

Standing at the head of the table, Mother Alphonsine led the novices in the grace before meals.

Then, moving sideways to avoid bumping into each other, the novices pulled out their stools and sat down. Three, including Sister Lucy, flopped to their knees. Kneeling during a meal was one of the regular penances, and each novice performed it two or three times a week. It was a good penance, to Sister Lucy's way of thinking. When they had first come into the novitiate, Reverend Mother had given them instructions about not enjoying their food too much. Food was to be eaten for the good of one's health, to satisfy bodily needs, not for base pleasure.

Sister Felicity stood holding a book and facing Mother Alphonsine. The novice mistress nodded as the food, in white serving dishes, made its way down both sides of the table.

"In the name of the Father and of the Son and of the Holy Ghost," began Sister Felicity, making the sign of the cross. She opened the book. "*For Greater Things: The Story of St. Stanislaus Kostka.*"

Sister Lucy helped herself to mashed potatoes and meatballs swimming in dark brown gravy, and began to eat. From the corner of her eye she noticed plates on the sideboard holding generous slices of chocolate cake.

"'*It was a quiet, humble life, full of peace, near to God, hidden away from men,*'" Sister Felicity read. "'*In this life the novices had to continue for two years, before they took upon themselves the obligation of vows. During those two years they tested their vocation, making sure that God really called them to that life; and they tested their own wills to see if they were ready to endure what such a life demanded of them.*'"

Another twinge in Sister Lucy's neck caused her to wince, and she shifted her body. Her feet collided with the wall as they often did when she was kneeling at the table, and she put her fork down while she tried to manoeuvre her legs around each other.

"*'Stanislaus did just what the other novices did, nothing out of the ordinary. Yet, of course, he was different from the others; he was a saint. What was the difference? Just this: they did things more or less well; he did things perfectly. If he prayed, he put his whole mind and soul into his prayer. If he worked, he obeyed orders absolutely, because in doing so he was obeying God.'*"

When most of them had nearly finished their cake, Mother Alphonsine said, "praise be to Jesus," and Sister Felicity responded, "Amen, in the name of the Father and of the Son and of the Holy Ghost." Sister Felicity put the book on the sideboard, sat down and helped herself to meatballs. Forks scraped against plates as the novices finished the meal in silence.

Later, after the novices and postulants had completed their evening charges, they seated themselves again in the common room, their black sewing bags on their laps. Their faces were animated this time, with looks of expectation. Sister Camillus once again had a grin on her face. The evening's recreation hour was set to begin.

"Well, praise be to Jesus," said Mother Alphonsine, sweeping into the room, her rosary swaying, a wide smile on her face.

"Amen, good evening, Mother," they shouted. Several began to speak at once.

"Mother, Sister Camillus was certainly edified by the reading on conformity to the will of God," said Sister Felicity with a glint in her eyes. The novices never spoke directly to each other at recreation; they always addressed the novice mistress, but in fact their talk formed a sort of third-person dialogue directed at each other. Looking over at her, Sister Lucy wondered if the smile on Sister Felicity's face came from genuine mischief, or if it masked disapproval.

Several novices giggled. Sister Camillus looked around the group, a sly look on her face as if she might be trying to weigh the possibility of getting some fun out of *Practice of Perfection and Christian Virtue*. "Well you know, Mother," she answered slowly, "the woman was a holy conformer after all, and she probably helped poor St. Dominic with his libido."

Sister Lucy stiffened and lowered her head. She didn't know what libido meant, but the look in Sister Camillus's eyes and the collective intake of breath around the group made her feel that the novice had gone too far, that now the axe was going to fall. Sister Lucy hated that feeling.

"Does anyone have some jokes to tell us?" broke in Mother Alphonsine. Sister Lucy relaxed. This was the novice mistress's way of dealing with an embarrassing situation. She always seemed adept at changing the subject whenever the recreation topic became uncomfortable. Sister Lucy suspected that if she were let loose, Mother Alphonsine could tell a few jokes that weren't considered proper for novices' ears. As it was, she had to remain bland for the sake of edification.

Sometimes she tried to be stern, but sternness didn't become Mother Alphonsine, Sister Lucy thought. The sides of her mouth, which trembled when she tried to put on a serious face during a discussion of one of the readings or an instruction on the Holy Rule, gave her away. Sister Lucy thought she must dread the chapters that came at the end of each treatise of *Practice of Perfection and Christian Virtue*. Right now the group was stilled, as if the jokes, which the novices generally told and retold, always laughing as if for the first time, had suddenly dried up.

Sister Lucy spoke into the hush. "What if any of us gets sick, Mother? Is it better not to say anything, and let it get worse and worse, or is it better to ask to see the doctor? I mean, which is the best way of conforming to the will of God?" Sister Lucy could sense boredom on either side of her, a restless desire for someone to say something that would make them all laugh.

"Conformity to the will of God? I'll tell you about conformity to the will of God," came a booming voice from the back of the group. Sister Catarina was a hefty novice with black bushy eyebrows that continually rose and fell beneath the white band across her forehead. Right now she sat at a table tearing pages from a thick telephone directory and folding them neatly in half, then in thirds. Sister Catarina's after-supper charge included placing these papers, along with a supply of sanitary napkins, in the toilet cubicles of the convent washrooms. The purpose of the folded directory pages was to wrap used napkins.

"Conformity to the will of God is this: that the poor old nuns have the supplies they need at all times."

"The poor *old* nuns don't need them," laughed Sister Pauline. Once again, Sister Lucy stiffened. She herself would never have had the courage to say such a thing, but of course Sister Pauline could get away with a lot because she came from a family upon which God had set a special seal. Her parents had given all of their five children to God – their three sons had become Franciscan priests and another daughter had become a nun. Now Sister Pauline, their beloved baby, had made her parents' sacrifice complete by following in the others' footsteps and offering her life to God. Everyone else stood in wordless awe of her and her family. Fortunately, Sister Pauline didn't take herself as seriously as everyone else did; otherwise, Sister Lucy felt, she would have been too much to bear.

"Let me tell you this," Sister Catarina barged on. "Folding papers may not seem very important, but this is God's will for sure. When you need these things, you really need them." She paused for effect. "When my family asked me what I do all day, I told them I'm doing very important paperwork."

"Mother, is it possible to know at all times whether you are conforming to the will of God?" asked Sister Lucy. She was dying to get off the subject of sanitary napkins.

"Have you not been following the instructions on holy obedience, Sister Lucy?" Mother Alphonsine had kind blue eyes that rested above the rims of her glasses, and that now gazed on Sister Lucy. "Have you not remembered that the least wish of the superior is the command of the good religious?"

"The next section in the life of St. Stanislaus tells about how he was told to carry wood from a woodpile with another novice," said Sister Felicity. "They were told to carry two or three pieces each and the other novice wanted to carry an armload, but St. Stanislaus said, 'No, we were told to carry only two or three pieces, so that's the will of God for us.' I was wondering – do you think maybe he was just lazy and they turned the story around and made it look like he was virtuous?"

The thought of a saint being lazy intrigued Sister Lucy for a moment, but today's earlier reading about Bona and the worms refused to let go. "But Mother, how do you know if God wants your body to be eaten up by worms?"

"They're expecting more snow tonight, and so we'll have to shovel the walks tomorrow," said Mother Alphonsine, her eyes once again fixed on her embroidery. Sister Lucy looked over at Sister Camillus. The other novice's face was blank, her mouth open slightly. Her eyes, meeting Sister Lucy's, began to dance again and she stuck out her tongue, then bowed her head over a long darning needle that she plunged into a black stocking fitted over a mushroom-shaped form.

Later, at night prayers, as the Litany of Our Lady droned around her – ". . . House of Gold, pray for us, Spiritual Vessel, pray for us, Vessel of Honour, pray for us, Singular Vessel of Devotion, pray for us . . ." – Sister Lucy imagined a beautiful woman going about helping people, her face full of gentleness and quiet joy, while worms ate up her body. When night prayers were over, and the chapel was darkened except for a single light bulb at the back, a nun read the meditation passage for the next morning. "From the book of the Apocalypse, chapter 3. *'Thus says the Amen, the faithful and true witness, who is the beginning of the creation of God: I know thy works; thou art neither cold nor hot. I would that thou wert cold or hot. But because thou art lukewarm, and neither cold nor hot, I am about to vomit thee out of my mouth; because thou sayest, I am rich and have grown wealthy and have need of nothing, and dost not know that thou art the wretched and miserable and poor and blind and naked one . . .'"*

As soon as the scripture reading ended, Reverend Mother rang a little handbell from the place where she knelt at the back of the chapel. All the nuns and novices bent down and kissed the floor. Sister Lucy's neck gave a twinge of pain as she straightened. She then filed out of chapel with the others, up the staircase, past the novices' common room, to the dormitory.

She pulled the curtains around her cubicle and stood still for a moment. Beside her bed were a chair and a bedstand on which stood a basin and jug. Folded on top of the jug was her pink and white towel, placed there by the novice whose after-supper charge was to fill all the jugs with hot water. Sister Lucy pulled the plain white bedspread from the bed, folded it and placed it over the top of the chair. She unhooked her rosary from her belt, gathered it up in her palm and placed it beside her basin. Then, methodically, she began to take off her clothes, placing each item on the seat of her chair – her veil, dress, pockets and undervest. Covering her small breasts with one arm, she withdrew her nightgown from under the pillow and then pulled it over the top of her head. She began to undress the lower part of her body: her plain blue petticoat, her underpants. She undid the garters of her black stockings, removed them, and then finally unhooked her garter belt. She took off her undercap and smoothed back her short hair with her hand. She then poured the water, still warm, from the jug into the basin. She wet the washcloth, rubbed it with soap and began to wash, first her face and neck, and then, reaching into the top of her nightgown, under her arms and beneath her breasts. The moist thickness of the cloth felt soothing on her skin. After drying herself, she brushed her teeth, rinsing and spitting into the basin. She put her habit dress over her nightgown and carried the basin to the housemaid's sink in the corridor outside the dormitory. She refilled the basin and brought it back to her cubicle. The next morning, long after the water in the basin had grown cold, she would wash in it.

"Cold water is good for a person in the morning," Mother Alphonsine had said when explaining the dormitory procedures. "Besides," she added, "washing yourself with cold water is a nice penance to offer Our Lord first thing in the morning."

Sister Lucy wasn't exactly sure, from Mother Alphonsine's explanation, what the real reason was for washing with cold water every morning. Was it for reasons of physical well-being, or was it for penitential reasons? She suspected the real reason was one of expediency. In the scramble to get washed and dressed and to do the various charges that needed to be done in the half hour between rising and six o'clock meditation, it simply saved time for the novices to have water already in their basins.

After she had taken off her habit dress again, Sister Lucy knelt down beside her bed and stretched her arms to either side. This was the final penance of the day. Three times a week she knelt like this, reciting the Litany of Humility, in imitation of Jesus who had died with His arms outstretched on the cross. "That others may be loved more than I, Jesus grant me the grace to desire it; that others may be chosen and I set aside, Jesus grant me the grace to desire it; that others may be preferred to me in everything, Jesus grant me the grace to desire it . . ."

She pictured again the beautiful Bona, disfigured by her rotting breasts, smiling through her agony, happy to be suffering for the love of God. Her own aches were tiny in comparison. Imagine the festering breasts, the worms crawling in and out of the pus! She cringed at the thought, and with a jerk, her arms fell and fastened themselves in a tight hug around her body. Her own breasts felt firm against the pressure.

Her head twitched as pain shot up into her forehead. She slumped onto her heels, her arms falling limp on the bed. She couldn't do it. She couldn't suffer for the love of God as Bona had. She had given up everything to become a good religious, but what was she? Weak and mediocre, getting by from day to day. She would become more and more selfish, first in small things, then in greater things. She was lukewarm, that's what she was, one of those people whom Jesus, at the last judgment, will vomit out of His mouth.

She looked up through the crack between the dormitory curtains. In a space of about two inches, she saw Sister Pauline beside her own bed, kneeling erect with arms fully outstretched. Sister Lucy knelt upright again, then slumped forward, the crown of her head resting on the bed, her arms hanging limp at her sides. She felt exhausted and defeated. It was useless to try to become holy. She could never manage it, never.

For a moment, she thought of nothing, aware only of the rough comfort of the blanket under her head. Then she realized that her body was beginning to relax, the pain subsiding.

In a whisper she breathed out the final invocation of the litany: "That others may become holier than I, provided that I may become as holy as I should, Jesus grant me the grace to desire it."

The one-minute bell sounded. Sister Lucy stood up, leaning on the bed. She pulled down her bedclothes and climbed in between the sheets. Then she bunched up her pillow under her neck for traction and closed her eyes. Tomorrow, right after breakfast, there would be a chance to speak to Mother Alphonsine.

*Feast of the Purification*

THE PIECE OF CLOTH THAT SISTER GERALDINE pulled out of her black work bag was called a runner. She had never heard the term before entering the novitiate; her embroidery work had been confined to cross-stitched blue and green peacocks on pillowcases for her mother's birthday four or five years ago. Recently, one of the other novices, on Mother Alphonsine's orders, had taught her the long-and-short stitch. The result now lay on the dust cloth covering Sister Geraldine's lap: an outcrop of tangled orange and yellow embroidery threads rising from a crumpled piece of linen, rather than the smooth likeness of a poppy that was supposed to be there.

Sister Geraldine would have preferred to stick with the cross-stitch. So what if it was overly simple? But Mother Alphonsine, the novice mistress, had said no, master the long-and-short stitch, and when it's done well enough, then we can even move on to cut-work. Mother had spoken, and what was she, Sister Geraldine, here for but to learn obedience, and not just an okay, ho-hum obedience, but a wholehearted submission of her own will to the will of her superior, which manifested the will of God.

The midday hour-long recreation had just begun. In the novices' common room, the long brown table had been moved to the back to make space for a semicircle of sixteen wooden hard-backed chairs. The moments of silence just before recreation always bristled with a sense of eagerness as the chairs were quietly shuffled into position and smiles were exchanged in anticipation of talk just ahead. The twelve novices in white veils, wimples and black habits, and the four postulants in black capes and dresses, now sat facing Mother Alphonsine. All were plying needles to cloth. The novice mistress worked a thin crochet hook, creating something white and lacy. The group, excited to be speaking after a morning of silence, tended toward high-pitched chatter, all vying for the novice mistress's attention. Sister Geraldine had learned early on — just over a year ago, to be exact — that at recreation chatter and laughter were permitted and even encouraged, but one novice never spoke to another. There was one conversation, and all remarks were addressed to the novice mistress.

"There's less than a year to go now, Mother," said Sister Henriette. "This is the last day of January. So there are eleven more months to go before 1960. Starting today, I'll do the countdown." She widened her eyes

*Feast of the Purification*

and lifted her eyebrows, and the bandeau across her forehead gave a gentle rise into the whiteness of the wimple framing her face. "If I may, Mother."

"What's 1960, Sister?" Mother Alphonsine's eyes remained on the slender thread hooked around her small finger. Round wire-framed glasses sat halfway down her nose.

"Doesn't anyone remember, Mother?" the novice said, looking around. "The vision of Our Lady at Fatima! Her secrets! When she appeared to the three peasant children, she told them to pray for the conversion of Russia – that was just about the time Communism began, around 1917, wasn't it? – and then she told them a secret that wasn't to be revealed until 1960. So here we are, just about. Eleven more months."

"More to the point perhaps is that the day after tomorrow is the feast day of Purification Church, and it's also the first day of the parish bazaar," Mother Alphonsine said. "We'll have an hour of reading this afternoon for you to finish what you're working on. They're always the first things to sell, the pieces done by the nuns and novices – the tablecloths, the tray covers, the baby clothes. One of the women organizing the bazaar said to me yesterday, 'The Sisters' needlework is always beautifully done. Perfection!'"

"Actually, Mother, they say the Pope already knows the secret," Sister Geraldine said. "Well, not the new Pope, of course. The old Pope."

"The *former* Pope, Sister." Mother Alphonsine said. She looked over her glasses at Sister Geraldine. Her lips turned up into a gentle smile. "Or more precisely, the *late* Pope."

Sister Geraldine slipped a scabbard containing a pair of scissors from her pocket and clipped an orange thread close to the cloth. Mother Alphonsine's correction was a pinprick of humiliation, nothing more. It served her right. She didn't actually know whether Lucia, the only one of the three child visionaries who had survived to adulthood, had really told Our Lady's secret to the Holy Father. She was now just trying to show off, to let it be known that she knew as much as Sister Henriette did about these matters. So, yes, it served her right to be publicly corrected.

"Does anyone know the names of the children who saw Our Lady at Fatima, Mother?" one of the novices asked.

"Lucia, Jacinta and Francisco," came a chorus of voices around the room, followed by chattery laughter.

"Everything comes in threes in that part of the world, Mother," said another novice. "The Nina, the Pinta, and the Santa Maria!" Again, laughter.

"What do you think Our Lady's secret's going to be, Mother?" Sister Henriette asked.

Sister Geraldine looked over at her. The other novice was working the satin stitch. Her piece, stretched taut and held by an embroidery hoop, was covered in a splash of colours. Probably a bouquet of flowers or a garden scene. A lot of green appeared as well – leaves, perhaps, or a watering can. Her lips were pursed and her eyes fixed on the work in her hands as she turned it over and smoothed the underside. She seemed tense: was she unhappy with the way the topic was swerving into foolish talk?

A chorus of voices chimed in. "It's about the end of the world." "The new Pope said —" "Maybe there's more stuff about Russia and Communism."

Mother Alphonsine looked up and smiled broadly now. "If there's a secret from Our Lady, we'll learn about it in God's good time. We know one thing for sure: there won't be anything more in it than we already know through Revelation."

The general movement of bodies and the shaking and nodding of heads had stilled, and the voices had trailed off once Mother Alphonsine had begun speaking. The room was still until someone said quietly, "And the Holy Father will only let us know what's good for us, won't he, Mother?"

"That's right. And speaking of that —" Mother Alphonsine unwound the thread from her finger and put down the crochet hook and the lacy piece. From the side of her desk she picked up a sheet of newspaper that had been neatly folded. She looked down through her glasses at the newspaper and then lifted her eyes to the group in front of her. "Our dear Pope John XXIII has announced that an ecumenical council will take place."

The group still sat somewhat subdued. Some put their needlework on their laps, seeming eager for more of this news. Sister Geraldine pulled hard on a thread at the back of the runner, then turned the piece over to smooth out the stitch. She actually wanted to hear more about the secret of Fatima.

"It says there have been only twenty councils in the history of the Church," Mother Alphonsine said, looking down through her glasses at the print. "The last council finished prematurely in 1870 because of the Franco-Prussian war, and this may be a continuation of that council. The Holy Father hasn't said yet."

"What does – what's that word again, Mother?" one of the novices asked. She had moved toward the edge of her chair, as if expecting something important.

"Ecumenical. Eck-you-*men*-ical." Mother Alphonsine gave a slight shrug and a look of amused self-deprecation. "I must admit it's not a word I'm altogether familiar with. Especially since the last council of its kind was almost a hundred years ago. And before that, the Council of Trent. Sixteenth century. A little before my time." She looked down at the sheet again. "It will have something to do with Christian unity. We must pray for the success of this council. That all may be one again."

"Who'll be going to this council, Mother?" asked the novice who was still sitting on the edge of her chair.

"Well, certainly the cardinals, I suppose. Perhaps some bishops. Those, of course, who have the best knowledge of the Church."

"Did Sister think the Holy Father might invite us?" said Sister Camillus from the far end of the semicircle. She deepened her voice, simulating a man's.

"Oh, Sister, tell us what you know about Church unity. Tell us how we should convert the Protestants."

"Well, Mother, if we'd had conversations with Our Lady, he might," Sister Geraldine said. The mood had shifted from the boring news about a council and had become lighthearted again. "Maybe they'll ask Lucia. She must be very holy after talking with Our Lady in Fatima all those years ago. She's still alive, isn't she, Mother?"

"Yes, Mother." Sister Henriette was quick on the mark. She laid down her needlework on her lap and counted on her fingers. "If she was twelve when Our Lady appeared in 1917, then she'd be – she'd be – fifty-four now."

"Lucia became a nun, didn't she, Mother?" Sister Geraldine said.

"Yes, Mother, a Carmelite. She's in a convent somewhere in Portugal," said Sister Henriette.

"Well, that would make sense, wouldn't it, Mother?" said Sister Geraldine. "Not that she's in Portugal, but that she's a nun. After you've actually seen Our Lady and heard her speak, there's nothing else to do afterwards except to dedicate your whole life to God."

Voices around her murmured politely.

"I wonder if the other nuns consider her a saint, Mother," said Sister Camillus.

"She must be, Mother," Sister Geraldine said. "It must be easier for her to conform to the Holy Rule in all things because she's actually known Our Lady personally. It must make a difference."

"The difference might be that she's a pain to live with – if she's ultra-holy, that is," said Sister Camillus.

"Now, Sister." Mother Alphonsine spoke into her lace, a mild rebuke. Sister Camillus returned her concentration to her own work.

Sister Geraldine kept on: "If the story's true, Mother, that Lucia actually spoke to the Pope and told him Our Lady's secret, what do you think it was like to settle back into the convent routine and being anonymous and submitting your will and all that, after she'd actually told heavenly secrets to the Pope himself? Everyone would be bowing and scraping –"

"Speculation is useless," said Mother Alphonsine. Her voice seemed unusually sharp. "And besides, with this new council coming up, the Pope has more important things to do than bother himself about secrets. These are not the things that matter."

"Yes, Mother." Another humiliation. Sister Geraldine looked down at the tangled threads on her lap.

"Time, Mother." The novice who had the job of bell-ringer, marking out the daily schedule, stood up, having pulled from inside her bodice a pocket watch attached by a black string to the inside of her habit. This was the signal to end recreation. Any indication from authority that the time was up for a given activity marked a signal from God that the activity must not continue for even a second longer. This was a matter of holy obedience. Some saint had once said that if one is writing, one is to stop in the middle of forming a letter when the bell rings. This was God's will. So a half-written *x,* for example, must be left with only one stroke and the second stroke, the one that crosses it, will have to wait until the next day, or whenever holy obedience dictates the writing activity to be taken up again.

Sister Geraldine felt only half sorry that recreation had come to an end. It truly was, in a way, fun (although it would be hard to explain this to her friends in the world). On the other hand, the knots in her embroidery were impossible to undo and there was little satisfaction in seeing the creation of a poppy petal that made the linen pucker up. Besides, there was still some white showing through where it should have been solid colour by now. This runner was going to be one sorry mess, definitely unfit for the parish bazaar. Nor would it find its way into the visitors' parlour, nicely starched and ironed to perfection, its poppies brightly blinking at either end while a potted plant of real flowers sat in the middle. All in all, she was glad to wrap the thing up in her dust cloth and bundle it into her work bag.

Sister Henriette, of course, was the first off the mark at the end of recreation. Even before Mother Alphonsine intoned, "Praise be to Jesus," in response to the bell-ringer, Sister Henriette had folded her work and wrapped it tightly, leaving not a wrinkle in her dust cloth. She was the first to rise, the first to lift her chair, and whereas the other chairs scraped against the floor in spite of novices' efforts at silence, her movements were noiseless except for the muffled sound of her rosary beads knocking against each other within the folds of her serge habit skirt.

Sister Geraldine and Sister Henriette had been the two religious vocations to emerge from the 1957 graduating class of St. Monica's. Henriette, or Henny as everyone called her, had been the popular class president in their final year. At the end of the school day, when the girls burst out of the front door, Henny was always the girl whom the St. Paul's boys, their ties loosened and their three-ring zippered binders tucked under their arms, loped toward with wisecracks and grins. She wore the burgundy school uniform as stylishly as possible, pushing up the sleeves of her sweater just so, revealing the tan on her hands and forearms in a disarming way, daring even to wear lipstick sometimes. Sister Geraldine had even seen her cheat on a Religion exam one day, lifting the top of her desk when the presiding nun wasn't looking, and flipping through the pages of the textbook.

Toward the end of the final year, Henny had begun to change. She joined Our Lady's Sodality and pledged herself as a Child of Mary on the day of the May procession. She still maintained her stylish, tanned appearance, her silky hair and her easy quips with the boys, but she also wore her Child of Mary medal with pride, letting it dangle from her neck on its blue cord in full view. Then she had given the class speech at the communion breakfast the morning following their graduation. Looking confidant, her pretty dark hair in a long flow with an up-flip at the ends that Sister Geraldine had never been able to master,

*Feast of the Purification*

Henny had said, "The future is ours, and each one of us must answer before God as to the vocation He is calling us to." Or words to that effect. Something in Sister Geraldine had stirred, and although Henny was dating the class valedictorian from St. Paul's – it was the romance the whole school talked about – she knew that Henny was considering a vocation to the religious life: the call to give up everything and to follow where God was leading. And that same day – it wasn't just that she looked up to Henny with a mixture of envy and admiration because of her hair and her boyfriend – Sister Geraldine knew the vocation that she herself was to follow. She wanted to be a popular teacher, like Sister Zelie or Sister Barbara, but of course had learned since then that popularity was nothing but a trap. She would eventually become a teacher and thus, of course, would be called to love her students – or more precisely, to love Christ in them. But first of all she was called to a life of perfection as lived in the vows of poverty, chastity and obedience.

And the most difficult, in spite of what anybody in the world thought, was obedience. It meant giving up one's whole will, not just outwardly, but inwardly and joyfully, as in the case of the monk who watered a dry stick in the ground for a whole year because his superior told him to, not saying what a stupid thing to do, what a waste of time, the stick is dead, it's not going to grow. No, watering the stick as if it were a precious plant, green and alive.

"Mother, the minor key seems so sad for a happy feast day. Why can't we sing something that's joyful and in three parts?" It was not usual for a novice to speak out like this at choir practice, but Sister Geraldine was feeling disgruntled; it was her favourite time of the day, this half hour when the novices gathered in the basement music room to practise the hymns for the coming masses. They'd had the extra reading hour earlier and most of the novices had handed in their needlework. Only the postulants and Sister Geraldine had nothing to offer for the bazaar. But at least, she thought, there would be some beautiful music for Our Lady's feast. Again, they sat in a semicircle, only this time they faced the upright piano and Mother Estelle, who sat on the stool before it. The late afternoon light suddenly cast a gloom upon the room.

"No, no, no, no, *no!*" Mother Estelle swivelled around to face the group, her rosary clattering against the stool. She wore round, thick eyeglasses that made Sister Geraldine think of cylindrical ice cubes. "In Gregorian chant you forget major and minor. Forget *harmony.*" She seemed to blink behind her spectacles. "Forget your popular songs. Forget Western music entirely. This music is more like that of the East. Now where are our spiritual origins?" She looked back and forth across the tops of the novices' heads. "Where?"

"In the Bible." The answer came faintly from the edge of the group.

"Sacred Scripture. Right. First of all, the Hebrews of the Old Testament. And when the ancient Hebrews

*Feast of the Purification*

expressed their faith in song, it was –" She stopped, as if expecting an answer.

No one spoke. Sister Geraldine's mouth felt dry. Another slap in the face. She wished she had kept her mouth shut. But Gregorian chant, compared with the lush choral music they usually sang, bored her. She looked over at Sister Henriette. As usual, the other novice was sitting upright, her back unsupported. This position was, she presumed, a penance that Sister Henriette had set herself; a small mortification of the flesh. Sister Geraldine felt an urge to push her into the back of the chair, to pin her there, to tie her up, to bind up her mouth. She adjusted her gaze away from the other novice. It was important to dismiss such urges immediately as the work of the devil. But still – where had it come from? Had she placed herself in competition? Was Sister Henriette more obedient, was she turning into a better nun, sailing from a stylish and breezy life in school into an effortless life in the novitiate, calmly learning the ways of becoming a saint? Sister Geraldine couldn't remember how well she had done on the Religion exam that Sister Henriette had cheated on, and she certainly had never learned Sister Henriette's grade. They had never been friends, after all; Sister Henriette floating in the stratosphere of the popular crowd and Sister Geraldine clinging to the raft of girls with limp hair and pimples, like herself.

"It was Semitic chant," said Mother Estelle. She spoke in a matter-of-fact, resigned tone, as if she was used to answering her own questions. "Eastern. No major and minor, no treble and bass. Now." She turned back to the piano and let the fingers of her plump right hand fall on the keys. "Gregorian chant was created in *modes. Modes.* This is not a lesson in the theory of Latin chant, we have no time for that, but you must know that we don't sing it like Palestrina, or like modern songs that have emotion flying all over the place." She lifted her arms and waved them up and down, her sleeves flapping like wings. "The joy is expressed in the words themselves. Now." She brushed a key with her thumb. "The tract: *Nunc dimittis servum tuum.* 'Now you can let your servant go.' The prophet Simeon's great song of surrender. He sees the infant Jesus, and he sees His immaculate mother presenting herself to be purified, and he says, 'This is what I have lived for, and I now give it back to God.'" She let her arms dangle by the sides of the piano stool, then straightened and dropped her hand back onto the keys.

FEAST DAY OR NOT, Monday was radiator-dusting day in the chapel. As usual, Sister Geraldine started from Our Lady's side of the sanctuary. She would work her way down the side aisle, across the back, up the other side aisle, and finish on St. Joseph's side. The difference today was that Our Lady's altar was alive with carnations and roses. Three vigil lights danced before the statue's blue veil and her outstretched hands and the snake beneath her feet. Dressed now in her white cotton work habit, her white veil tied behind her shoulders, Sister Geraldine worked the green feather duster down between the warm sections of the sanctuary radiator. She didn't mind this duty: the duster reminded her of peppermint candy floss, and there was something satisfying in occasionally bringing out a large piece of fluffy dust – a satisfaction that reminded her of squeezing a pimple in the days when she was younger, those long-ago days in the world, when she examined her face in the mirror all she wanted, the days before she had been taught to practise mortification. Being happy to see a piece of fluff – proof that she was keeping the chapel clean – was surely an innocent pleasure, though, part of the hundredfold that God had promised.

The sanctuary radiator finished, she opened the gate of the communion rail and stepped down. A sound from the back of the chapel gave her a start; she immediately recognized the figure at the back as that of a novice; the white veil over the shoulders. What was happening? The novices and postulants had cleaning charges at this time; they were scattered all over the convent: in the dormitory and linen room and common room, in the infirmaries, the kitchen, the front and back stairs, the parlours. No novice except herself should be in the chapel just now. She felt self-conscious, pushing the feather duster in, pulling it out, in and out, bent down, then kneeling, lifting her skirt and exposing her black-stockinged knees to the floor. The floor was hard and cold. Who was it there at the back? Was it a moan that she had heard, like a baby's whimper?

Finally, the farthest radiator in the back on Our Lady's side of the chapel. Sister Geraldine tried to look straight ahead, at the narrow boards of the hardwood floor, at the edges of the pews, at the radiator slats. She tried to remember the meditation that accompanied today's Gospel reading. Jesus's mother and father — that was how the Scripture referred to them: his mother and father, not stepfather, not father substitute, not pretend father, but *father.* Our Lady — hearing that, a sword would pierce her heart. "What a sorrow for poor Mary," Mother Estelle had said at choir practice, her mouth turned down at the corners like that of a sad-faced clown. Sister Geraldine jabbed the handle of the duster into her chest. Her breastbone sounded hollow. She crouched before the radiator and pushed the duster in between the first two slats, peering into the darkness of it. Anna the prophetess who lived in the temple day and night. Would she have had her own room, with a cot and a bedside table? Living in the temple could have been quite comfortable, perhaps, not having to get up and go at the sound of the bell the whole day long. Being a prophetess, every time you opened your mouth people would look at you with respect, perhaps with a paper and pencil in their hands to write down the things you uttered.

It would be a superb act of penance for her now to keep her eyes firmly downcast, not to look to see who the novice was kneeling there, an act she could relate to Mother Alphonsine when permissions day came around. She was now abreast of the pew just in

*Feast of the Purification*

front of where the novice knelt. Sister Geraldine shifted to a crouching position, like a duck waddling on webbed feet. It was a better way in which to dust the radiator: approaching the dark spaces from a sideways fashion rather than head-on. But a cramp was forming in her leg and she really had to stretch it. Straightening up with her face toward the other novice would not mean that she was deliberately looking at her; it would simply mean that she had to straighten, that she just happened to be facing in that direction. If she became cramped and keeled over, or became stuck on her haunches, the dusting wouldn't get done and she therefore wouldn't be performing her charge as obedience dictated. It was better to stretch her leg and keep doing her work in obedience than it was to perform the act of mortification by remaining crouched and thereby avoid finding out who the novice was, now inches away from her.

Before thinking further, she stood up and shook her leg, facing the other novice.

It was Sister Henriette. Her posture was as upright, as perfect, as usual, and Sister Geraldine was struck by the graceful look of her, her white veil perfectly arranged over her shoulders. She was gazing straight ahead. Sister Geraldine took a quick glance toward the chapel door. The rest of the chapel was still, the empty brown pews and the distant Stations of the Cross like a painting or a frieze, a backdrop lacking in life. Sister Geraldine picked up the duster and dropped back onto her haunches. She sidled toward the other novice, running the duster around the seat and bending over to make it look as if she was catching the dust in the spot where the hinge connected the kneeler to the pew in front of it. "What are you doing?" She mouthed the words, her lips exaggerating the articulation.

The other novice stared at her. Her eyes, which were beadier and more closely set than Sister Geraldine had noticed before, narrowed slightly, and there was an involuntary twitch of her mouth. "What does it look like I'm doing?" Sister Henriette's voice seemed to boom inside the cavernous silence of the chapel. "I'm waiting for Our Lady to smile at me again."

Sister Geraldine shifted, still crouching, and planted her feet on either side of the kneeler. Her body felt wooden, and a knot began to form somewhere inside, between her solar plexus and her stomach. It felt hard, like a giant walnut. She noticed that the other novice's hands were held in a tight clasp, the knuckles stretched against the skin. Her lips were parted in a slight smile.

"It happened at prayers last night. The sanctuary was dark, and there were just those blue votive lights in front of Our Lady, and there was a kind of glow on the flowers, and she suddenly smiled."

Sister Geraldine turned and looked up at the altar of Our Lady. There was no movement in the painted face beneath the blue veil. She waited for the other novice to continue.

"You don't have to be a peasant girl in a grotto for Our Lady to show herself to you. It can happen in a convent chapel too. Look at St. Catherine Labouré and the miraculous medal."

Sister Geraldine coughed and swallowed hard. She sometimes coughed and sneezed when she was dusting, and she wasn't sure whether it was the dust in the air or Sister Henriette's unusual assertion that had made its way to her throat.

Sister Henriette's hands remained tightly clasped. "Can I help it if she smiled at me? Can I help it if she was just starting to speak when the bell rang at the end of night prayers? I did what I was supposed to do: I spoke to Mother Alphonsine about it and asked her if I might stay in chapel for the rest of the night. That's what I felt Our Lady wanted me to do: to keep vigil, to listen to what she had to say. To hear what she was telling me."

"What did she say?" Sister Geraldine was aware that she was beginning to break silence. "Mother Alphonsine, I mean." She wanted to move away, but couldn't. She seemed rooted to where she stood, cramped and crouching, straddling the kneeler in front of where Sister Henriette knelt, one hand on the worn seat of the pew, the other clutching the feather duster. She tried to speak again, but her lips merely moved up and down, feeling rubbery at the corners where the saliva gathered.

"What do you think she said? She said I had to go to bed, like everyone else. She thinks everybody should go around obeying the Rule all the time. She has no idea what it's like having Our Lady's statue come to life and smile at you and actually speak to you." She looked hard at Sister Geraldine, as if imploring her to do something. "That's why I'm here, why I couldn't go to my charge. Our Lady said to come to chapel, that she'd show herself to me again."

Sister Geraldine wished that Mother Alphonsine would come in and whisk the novice away in her usual discreet manner. She herself would be found out, however, the novice mistress's piercing eyes registering the kind of disapproval that Sister Geraldine always shrank from. It would be better if Mother Estelle stepped into the chapel and gave Sister Henriette a hard stare and told her to get up, go to her charge and stop spouting religious nonsense.

She wasn't sure how she lifted herself up from her cramped haunches; perhaps it was the thought that one of the nuns might come in and see her talking. She darted down the aisle and across the width of the chapel, letting the feather duster alight over whatever she happened to be passing. If someone should come in, it would at least look as if she was completing her cleaning rather than making a getaway. Before closing the sacristy door, she looked back at Sister Henriette. The novice knelt perfectly still, gazing at the tabernacle, or perhaps at Our Lady's altar. Her white veil fell in graceful folds over her slender shoulders, her habit sleeves perfectly in place. A doubt seized Sister Geraldine. Was she perhaps really having a vision?

The talk about the Fatima secret at recreation two days earlier came back to her now; she had forgotten it in the meantime, with all the fuss about the bazaar and with this morning's High Mass and the bacon and egg breakfast in honour of Our Lady's feast day. Her legs felt shaky as she put away the duster. She walked past the chapel door, genuflected and peered inside. The white-veiled figure still knelt in perfect formation, the sleeves draping beautifully downwards.

"SISTER HENRIETTE HAS LEFT US," said Mother Alphonsine just before recreation was to begin. "She has decided to return home to her parents. Let's all pray for her. Life is not easy in the world."

The semicircle of novices and postulants sat motionless and subdued. Work bags remained unopened.

Mother Alphonsine spoke into the silence somewhat reluctantly, Sister Geraldine thought. "There are many signs of a religious vocation. One of the important signs is a desire to follow the dictates of holy obedience. This is the surest way to know God's will. Following one's own private inclinations is not the way of obedience."

The group remained still, and even when recreation had begun, the voices in the room sounded flat and forced. The atmosphere would lighten over the next hour, however, and by the end of recreation the common room would be bursting with the usual excited chatter. Mother Alphonsine would tell amusing details about the parish bazaar. Sister Henriette's name would never be mentioned again.

Sister Geraldine thrust a darning mushroom into the toe of a black stocking. She enjoyed darning; it provided great satisfaction after relatively little work. Perhaps by some miracle the runner and its tangle of embroidery threads, if left untouched long enough at the bottom of her bag, might just disappear.

## *Composition of Place*

OUTSIDE, LIGHT FROM THE CHAPEL WINDOWS caught the dirty snow piled up along the eastern extension of the convent. Long icicles hung down from the roof like a row of dark spears. February was just about the worst month of the year.

And tomorrow was Ash Wednesday. That said it all. It meant that for the whole of Lent there was nothing immediate to look forward to, like flowers in the chapel and chocolate at Sunday tea and three-part motets at Benediction. Everything nice seemed so far away. Sister Lucy took a deep breath and let it out by parting her lips slightly rather than heaving a sigh as she would have liked. She pulled her attention back into the room.

The eleven novices and four postulants sat in a semicircle on straight-backed chairs, each in a long black habit and white veil. They held their bags of needlework on their laps and looked around at each other with smiles of anticipation. Facing them at the top of the room was a schoolteacher's desk, on which sat the black bag that contained the novice mistress's needlework. Sister Lucy usually loved this moment of expectation just before the beginning of recreation. This evening, however, she opened her needlework bag without enthusiasm and spread her flowered dust cloth across her lap.

Footsteps sounded outside the door, and the novices turned and rose to their feet. Mother Alphonsine swept into the room in a swish of black serge, the rosary that hung from her belt swinging from side to side. She wore the black veil of the professed nun.

"Praise be to Jesus," she said, smiling and making her way to her desk.

"Amen! Good evening, Mother," the novices sang in a giggly chorus that always reminded Sister Lucy of a bursting dam whenever the novice mistress gave this signal that they could talk. Mother Alphonsine looked like she was continuing to say something, but the sound of chairs scraping against the floor and the chorus of voices drowned her out.

"Those pancakes at supper, Mother," said Sister Mary Alma. "A sure sign, wouldn't you say? We're fattened up now for the rigours of Lent." She looked around the group. "Are we ready for the forty days in the desert, the fasting and penance?"

Mock groans sounded around the semicircle. Sister Lucy bent over the leaf she was embroidering in long-and-short stitch, light green against dark. The cloth was puckered at the edge of the stitching. She wasn't sure she wanted to laugh along with the others about something she dreaded so much; Lent meant plain hymns and a drab chapel without flowers, uninteresting meals with butterless bread and milkless tea and morning meditations on the suffering and death of Jesus. "In meditating on the death of Jesus we learn something about life," the novice mistress had told the novices during her instruction earlier in the day. "It's one of those Christian paradoxes that can't be explained." The instruction had left Sister Lucy feeling empty.

"We're not as strict as some orders, you know," Mother Alphonsine was saying now. She was working a crochet hook through a piece of white lace. "The Trappestines have very strict Lenten fasts, and so do the Carmelites. As a matter of fact, you could say that the Carmelites live a kind of Lent all year round. They always sing only the plainest of chants, even on Easter Sunday, the day when we outdo ourselves in making glorious music. And of course each Carmelite meditates before a skull in her cell every day. How would you like to have *that* reminder of your death every day of your life?" She stopped, and then threw up her hands, pretending to be shocked at herself. "But my goodness, why are we talking about such things at recreation? You'd think we weren't going to eat for the next forty days!"

"In school we used to have fortunes inside our pancakes on Shrove Tuesday," said Sister Felicity. "I remember mine two years ago said, 'You will meet someone tall and dark who will change you forever.' Is this Jesus, do you suppose? Or a new priest in confession?"

"Maybe it refers to Reverend Mother," said Sister Mary Alma with a straight face. "She's tall. And wears dark clothes. And what do you suppose she will say that will change you forever? She lowered her voice a tone and shifted her body into a stiff position. 'I'm sending you to Timbuktu, my dear Sister. To teach the pagans and convert sinners in the deepest, darkest regions of nowhere.'"

Sister Lucy laughed in spite of her gloom. She liked the silly talk at recreation. An intense silence, which flowed from early morning meditation and Mass, filled the rest of the day. They had been instructed to carry in their minds throughout the day the images and prayers from their meditation, so that at every moment, as they dusted furniture or peeled vegetables or washed dishes, their thoughts were supposed to be lifted to the things of God. One could get into trouble thinking about God all the time, however, and Sister Lucy's face burned whenever she remembered the time Sister Cook had upbraided her for leaving dried bits of porridge on the sides of a pot. She had been gazing at the crooked, water-stained picture of St. Anne and Our Lady above the sink as she swished the wash rag around the pot. Our Lady was about six years old in the picture. She was golden haired, held a book in one hand and a lily in the other, and already wore a halo. Drying the pot,

Sister Lucy thought about herself at the age of six, dressing her dolls and making mud pies, knowing nothing about God. Then, as she watched the dishwater swirl down the drain, wondering what things Our Lady would be thinking about at that moment, the cook, who had a temper, thrust the pot at her and told her to clean the blessed thing properly. It wasn't too much to ask of a novice, was it, that a simple pot be scraped clean? The cook's words hung in the air as Sister Lucy's eyes stung with tears and her small piece of steel wool scratched against the dried porridge on the inside of the pot. Sometimes everything was so hard.

But at recreation they laughed and talked nonsense. Although she herself was always a little afraid to speak out much lest she say the wrong thing, she loved the easy laughter and felt an anxious thrill whenever Sister Mary Alma used slang words that weren't allowed, like "darn," or skirted the edges of what seemed proper to talk about. Like the time she had said, "Mother, does anyone know the joke about Jesus and the woman caught in adultery?" Sister Lucy had stiffened and sucked in her breath, but Mother Alphonsine had simply looked over the top of her glasses at the novice and said, "Edification, Sister, edification," and had smoothly changed the topic, telling the group about some boring old thing the bishop had just written in the diocesan paper.

"What if," said Sister Mary Alma now, still carrying on, "the tall dark stranger is the devil-l-l –" she lengthened the word dramatically – "tempting you?"

THE NEXT MORNING Sister Lucy knelt briefly at the back of the chapel. Around her, the others – nuns, novices and postulants – were also kneeling, in no particular order, and then each in turn bent forward to kiss the floor before getting up and moving on to her place. Sister Lucy bent and touched her lips to the polished wood of the floor. A faint smell of paste wax mingled in her nostrils with the tingling sensation of dust. She breathed a sigh of relief that she wasn't on the chapel cleaning charge and thus wouldn't be the one to hear from Mother Alphonsine about the poorly mopped floor. Then she stood and walked up the side aisle. A bare light bulb burned at the back. The rest of the chapel was dim, and at the top the sanctuary was in darkness except for the shadows cast by the red sanctuary lamp hanging in front of the altar, and the votive lamps that flickered at the side altars of Our Lady and St. Joseph. The main altar stood bare, devoid of flowers, and even in the dim light Sister Lucy could tell that the curtain covering the tabernacle was a dull purple, the colour of penance and mourning. The colour of Lent.

Normally, Sister Lucy loved this early part of the day. Every morning at five thirty the shrill sound of an electric bell rang through the corridor outside the dormitories. In the novices' dormitory, the novice whose bed was closest to the light switch bounded up at the sound of the bell, turned on the light and called out, "Praise be to Jesus." All around the dormitory, muffled by sleep and the white curtains that separated the beds, came the response, "Amen," as feet hit the floor. She couldn't honestly say she liked that particular moment of springing out of bed, but once she was up she felt happy. She loved the early morning silence, the hushed sound of nuns hurrying to morning prayer and meditation, the darkened corridors and the grey winter light of the chapel. She loved the prayer of adoration in the silence of her own heart, followed by a kiss on the floor. It was an earthy act, humble and simple. The whole early morning ritual reminded her of the early Christians making their way to the catacombs of Rome in the dead of night.

Today, however, was Ash Wednesday, and the flatness she had felt inside yesterday evening remained. It was as if there was no joy or beauty anywhere; everything was drab and colourless. At the end of Mass the nuns and novices would file up to the communion rail, where the priest would move from one to another dipping his thumb into a crystal dish of black ashes, his wide purple vestment like a board against his back, white sparse hair limp on his head. His thumb would inscribe a gritty cross just below the white band that stretched across each forehead as he mumbled, "*Memento, homo, quia pulvis es, et in pulverem reverteris.*" *Remember, man, that thou art dust and unto dust thou shalt return.* Sister Lucy sighed and knelt down at her place, looking ahead at the bare and darkened sanctuary.

When morning prayers were finished, the reading of the first point of meditation began. A nun, standing at the back of the chapel under the burning light bulb, read from a meditation book in a voice that was clipped and precise. "*Place yourself with Adam at the moment of his condemnation, as he hears the humiliating words, Dust thou art and unto dust thou shalt return.*"

Sister Lucy tried to picture Adam and Eve leaving Paradise. "We always begin our meditation," Mother Alphonsine had said, "by establishing the composition of place — that is, we use our imaginations to place ourselves in the middle of the scene." From the time she had first heard the story of Adam and Eve, Sister Lucy had always pictured Paradise as the backyard of her family's home. The tree of good and evil from which the pair had eaten the forbidden fruit was the large oak tree that had cast shade over the lawn in the summer, had served as home base for hide-and-seek, and had been the place where every spring a robin's nest appeared. She saw Adam and Eve, heads bowed, getting up from a spot under the tree, walking out the gate of the backyard, wearing leaves as clothes, their hair long and unkempt, their faces and limbs covered with dirt. *Unto dust thou shalt return.* She looked at the dark sanctuary, the dull purple of the tabernacle curtain, the shadows cast by the vigil lights. There was nothing else to think about. What a shallow meditation. What if Mother Alphonsine asked her about it during the instruction period today? She would have nothing impressive to reveal. She thought back to yesterday's meditation review.

The meditation review always occurred during the novice mistress's morning instruction. The long table, which had been moved to the back of the room during recreation, now stood in its normal position, stretching down from the novice mistress's desk. The novices and postulants sat on either side of the table, their heads bowed and their hands folded on their laps. Yesterday, as Mother Alphonsine talked, Sister Lucy had looked, as she usually did, at the patterns in the brown oilcloth covering the table. A configuration of dots in front of her formed a straight line that ended in the join of two curves. It reminded her of the pipe stuck in between the toothless gums of the cartoon character Popeye the Sailor Man. Another curve of dots underneath could be taken to form his soft jowls. She remembered how she and her younger brother Charlie used to fight over the Sunday comics after the nine o'clock Mass, often tearing the pages in their tussle so that the pieces had to be spread on the floor and placed together like a jigsaw puzzle. A small series of dots above Popeye's pipe now looked for all the world like the outline of his sailor cap. She wondered why she hadn't noticed him in the oilcloth before.

Mother Alphonsine's voice had just then broken into her thoughts: "Will someone now please review a meditation from last week." Sister Lucy could feel the novice mistress's eyes moving down one line and up the other. She clenched her hands together in her lap. "Sister Geraldine," Mother Alphonsine intoned.

Sister Lucy relaxed and, her head still bowed, glanced across the table at the novice who had just been singled out. Sister Geraldine had a pale, expressionless face that reminded Sister Lucy of a plaster cast. Her chin receded into the folds of linen underneath.

"Mother, the meditation I remember from last week was on the healing of the woman with the discharge of blood, from chapter 8 of St. Luke." Sister Geraldine had turned in her chair to face the novice mistress. Her eyes widened, and her voice was intense.

"The crowd around Jesus is huge, and they're all trying to get close to Him to hear what He has to say, so they're kind of jostling each other, and you can imagine that He's having trouble walking, just getting ahead, with all the people on all sides of Him." She paused.

"Yes, I like the sound of this. Go on," said Mother Alphonsine.

"And then there's this woman who barges up to Him. And, Mother, can you imagine what it must have been like for her? She sees Jesus ahead of her. He's an important man, too important for her to talk to. Maybe she's a peasant woman, of a lower class. Maybe she's not very well educated and doesn't know what to say. Maybe no one knows about her disease. Or else maybe it's impossible to control and she always has embarrassing bloodstains that she can't do anything about – you know, Mother?" Sister Geraldine's face looked pleading, as if she was desperate to convince the novice mistress.

"Thank you, Sister. That is a very vivid composition of place," said Mother Alphonsine. She sounded less enthusiastic than she had been earlier. Sister Lucy tried to keep her head bowed, but her eyes were riveted on the other novice's face.

"And Mother –" Sister Geraldine continued to look over at the novice mistress, "– well, she has these embarrassing bloodstains, and, well, you know, a lot of women have trouble with their periods when they get older. They have a heavy flow, and there's a lot of pain sometimes. I know because my mother had a lot of trouble with it, and I bet that's what this woman had —"

"Thank you, Sister," Mother Alphonsine interrupted.

Sister Geraldine's pale face had become flushed and animated. "You can just imagine, Mother, how hard it would be to ask a man for help for that kind of a problem. Not only that, but in those days women were considered impure during menstruation. So she should have been an outcast, and yet here she goes and creeps up behind Jesus, she manoeuvres her hand through the crowd of people and she touches His cloak."

"Yes, Sister." Mother Alphonsine clipped the end of each syllable, her tone sharp.

Sister Lucy watched Sister Geraldine's face as it receded once again with an impassive expression into the folds of linen. She had been gripped by Sister Geraldine's meditation review. Try as she might to make up vivid compositions of place in her meditations, hers were flat in comparison. Listening to the other novice, she felt that she was right there in the crowd with Jesus and the suffering woman. But obviously Mother Alphonsine hadn't liked the way Sister Geraldine went on and on about the woman's blood. It was best to stick with Jesus Himself, keeping the meditation focused on Him, trying to see the expression on His face and the look in His eyes, trying to watch His actions and hear His words.

But Jesus didn't appear in today's meditation. She sat down, stared at the tabernacle curtain for a few moments and then knelt again. *Dust thou art and unto dust thou shalt return.* What more could she do with it? How long did it take for a human body to become dust? She thought about her grandmother, now dead a year, lying in her coffin beneath the ground, her skin disintegrating, the eyes gone, the bones revealed, maggots crawling in and out of the body that had once been warm, that had held her as a small child. Her grandmother's clothes had likely disintegrated too, all worldly vanity torn and eaten by the small creatures of the earth, leaving only naked, rotting flesh. She shuddered and sighed deeply, blinking a few times. It was a morbid thought, but what else was there to think about on Ash Wednesday, that day above all others when you think about your own death and your decaying body that one day will be nothing but dust? She breathed a prayer of thanks that she had come here, to this place, where she was surrounded by nuns who vowed themselves to loving God and praying for the world. But today, even the glorious thought of heroism wasn't enough to lighten the grey prospect of Lent.

For the rest of the day they went about their tasks with the sign of ashes on their foreheads, and every time Sister Lucy looked at the others she noticed the dirty smudge between their eyebrows, the sign of their deaths. She felt hungry all day; although their midday dinner was a normal-sized meal, they'd had only a piece of bread for breakfast, and for supper only bread and cheese. But at least Mother Alphonsine had not asked for a meditation review.

"'JESUS WALKS *into the Garden of Olives to pray at the start of His Passion, and there, as He lies prostrate in agony, His sweat becomes as drops of blood trickling on the ground.*'" The nun reading the meditation points paused, her voice sounding precise and without expression from beneath the bare light bulb at the back of the chapel. "'*His agony was the more terrible and cruel because it was not the effect of physical exhaustion, but of an interior struggle between feeling and the will.*'"

Sister Lucy felt the stillness of the kneeling bodies around her. The points for meditation now, as Lent progressed, invited them all to follow the way of the cross, walking with Jesus step by step on the path to His death. The reader continued: "'*Imagine you see Him bathed in blood. Now beg for courage and perseverance in the spiritual combat.*'"

Sister Lucy knelt and stared awhile at the grey shadows cast by the early morning light in the sanctuary. It pleased her to have a concrete image of Jesus to think about. She pictured Him walking up the hill to the garden, the gnarled olive trees that she had seen in pictures giving the scene a dark and brooding cast.

She imagined herself describing the scene to Mother Alphonsine: "I see Jesus all alone in the garden, leaning against a rock, Mother. It's nighttime, so all you can see are dark shadows and Jesus in a sweat, and the sweat becomes blood, and you can see His face now covered with it. You know how it is when you're sweating, Mother, how you feel sticky all over, and since Jesus is kneeling on the ground, it's probably dusty, and the dust and grime are getting clogged into His face and hands, and there's the awful taste of it in His mouth, and His clothes are soaked with blood. The air is probably chilly, and when you get a chill with wet clothes, it's – well, you know what it's like, Mother. And there He is, all alone. His friends have abandoned Him, and He's reaching out to God. He's weeping, and His eyes are red and swollen, and tears are streaking down His face, and He's stretching out His hands that are covered with blood." It was a vivid meditation so far. Mother Alphonsine would like it.

The reader broke through Sister Lucy's musings. "'*This bloody sweat makes us understand what was passing in the soul of Jesus during His agony; how violent was the struggle; the battle between what He felt like and what He was being called to! See how great is His love that He would endure such things.*'"

Sister Lucy sat down. The reader's words echoed through her: the battle between what He felt like and what He was called to. What was she called to at this moment? She was called to sit with Jesus in His agony, knowing that He was heading toward death, clinging to the belief that His death contained the seeds of life. She felt lazy and worthless. In her meditation she had done nothing more than conjure up vivid imaginings of Jesus to impress Mother Alphonsine and the other novices. She was a charlatan and her meditation nothing but a sham. She was no better than Jesus's disciples who had been with Him in His agony, and yet still betrayed and abandoned Him. Of what use was her being in the convent, with the sacrifices and the monotony of it all and the repetitive and boring existence, where one strived for perfection and failed at every moment? What use was it if she did nothing but make a show of herself? She imagined the face of Jesus, His eyes looking at her with reproach through bloody strands of hair. It was too much. There was nothing she could do. She might as well forget about meditation. She was nothing but a pile of manure crawling with worms and maggots. She closed her eyes and again in her imagination saw the face of Jesus, the blood pouring out of Him now, and flowing over the small creatures that were making a feast of her body. His blood mingled with the blood of the woman with the hemorrhage, and the blood all flowed together, the blood drained out of her grandmother too. The pool of blood was rising, and into it flowed all the blood of everyone, everywhere, all in a struggle between feeling and will, between death and life, all mingled with the blood of Jesus. She swallowed and imagined the taste of blood in her mouth. And then she knelt.

She kept kneeling, her eyes fixed on the dull purple of the tabernacle curtain, until the overhead lights went on and the bell rang to signal the priest's arrival for Mass. Her body felt light, weightless.

"Sister Lucy?"

Sister Lucy lifted her eyes from the pattern of dots on the brown oilcloth. "Yes, Mother?"

"Can you tell us about your meditation this morning?"

Sister Lucy swallowed and glanced across at the still bodies facing her, their eyes downcast. "Well, Mother, Jesus was suffering in agony." She struggled to think clearly. Her mind had been on an itchy spot on the side of her face, inside where the starched linen wimple held firm against her cheek. "His sweat was like blood," she began. "He was praying on His knees." She stopped, trying to remember the reader's words from this morning's meditation, but there was nothing but blankness. She looked down at her hands. They were clenched, the fingers of each pressed into the palm of the other. Around her the novices sat motionless. The room was filled with silence. "He was, uh, He was in the Garden of Olives."

The table swam in front of her, a mass of brown liquid. She unclenched her hands and lay them loosely on her lap. "I'm sorry, Mother," she mumbled.

After a moment, Mother Alphonsine spoke. "No one, of course, knows what goes on between God and the soul during the time of meditation, but one thing is sure: we must put all our human faculties at God's disposal. We must try and use our imaginations better, Sister Lucy." There was a weary, pitying tone in the novice mistress's voice.

"Yes, Mother," said Sister Lucy. Her hands were now resting open and relaxed on her lap. She was surprised that Mother Alphonsine's rebuke washed through her with barely a ripple. She had seen Jesus suffering in the garden; she had really seen Him, and that was enough.

She looked back down at the brown oilcloth. Once again the patterns of dots were evident. One set of dots seemed to bear a faint resemblance to the head of another character from the comics, Dagwood Bumstead, several small dots forming lines like the two straight strands of his hair. Just below the dots were two dark spots that she imagined as Dagwood's oval-shaped eyes, set in perpetual astonishment. She thought of the crazy, clumsy things he was always doing – getting caught in the bathtub, diving down the clothes chute, making a mad dash for the morning bus with his shirttails flying.

For a brief second she smiled, then brought her mouth back into a straight line again, her face in serious repose.

## *Silence Pages*

"The box should say 'Passion,'" said Sister Geraldine. "Or maybe 'Purple cloths.'" She stood on tiptoe at the foot of the stepladder, stretching to see into the sacristy's high, deep storage cupboard. Her face, normally pale and withdrawn inside the stiffness of her white wimple, was now thrust upward, flushed, her chin jutting into the air. Her hands on either side clutched the blue apron that covered her white cotton work habit.

The postulant, whose name was Melanie, stood on the top of the stepladder, her torso now halfway into the cupboard. The full skirt of her long black dress and the edge of her blue apron swished gently against Sister Geraldine's face. The ladder itself stood tight against the flat surface below the cupboard, crushing the priest's Mass vestments that the two had laid out earlier. The vestments appeared as folds of bunched-up cloths of purple and white between the ladder's rungs.

"It's not here," said Melanie, speaking into the darkness of the cupboard.

"Purple cloths? Purple coverings? It has to be there. Where else could it be?" Sister Geraldine took a quick look around the sacristy, her eyes wide with anxiety. Apart from the vestments, the cruets in their little glass dish on the small side table, and the brass thurible stand on the floor beside the radiator, the room was empty of objects. She took shallow bursts of breath. "Passiontide? Passion Sunday?" Her mouth hung open and she blinked several times, her eyelids lined with short, light lashes. "Passion something or purple something. It has to be there."

"Lent?" Melanie brought her face to the front of the cupboard. Beneath the loose fit of the postulant's hairnet, her hair was dark brown and wavy. "Do you think they'd be in the Lent box?'

Sister Geraldine sighed in exasperated defeat. "Well, they shouldn't be. Lent is Lent and Passiontide is Passiontide, but let's see."

Melanie pulled a large box out from under a pile and, teetering on the top step of the ladder, handed it over in an awkward movement of arms, her cape awry and her skirt rustling. The box was covered with pale flowered wallpaper. Sister Geraldine held out both arms and carried it like a baby over to the sacristy table. She removed the lid and, looking at Melanie, pursed her lips and let out a low whistle. Her shoulders relaxed. She reached inside the box, gathered an armload of purple cloths and threw them in a pile on the table.

"What if we hadn't found them," she whispered.

There were three cloths in the pile. She held each one up, examining it briefly before dropping it again. They looked like three shapeless bags of varying sizes. She looked down at the purple heap and shifted the bandeau across her forehead, lifting her eyebrows with a slight grimace. She reached into her pocket and pulled out a small booklet made from the backs of envelopes and old greeting cards. The booklet had been roughly stitched up the centre, and a small pencil dangled from a string attached to the stitching. The cover had been cut from a piece of cardboard, and it bore, in her handwriting, the sentence, *The Sisters show their charity by their silence when they ought to keep it.*

She walked over to the corner of the sacristy toward the priest's wooden prie-dieu and chair. She sat down, leaned against the chair's high back and opened the pages.

Melanie watched as she did so, her mouth open. "I thought we weren't supposed to sit in the priest's chair," she said.

Sister Geraldine reddened and rubbed her lips together and stood up, holding the booklet in one hand and the pencil with its short string in the other. "It's just that you can't do this very well standing up."

Melanie clasped her hands together. "What is that?"

Sister Geraldine kept her eyes on the booklet, parted her lips, then closed them again. She let the pencil dangle as she massaged a rough spot on the cuticle of her forefinger. "I'm not supposed to tell you. They're silence pages." She scooped up the pencil and lowered her head in concentration. "You'll know when you're a novice." She glanced toward the door that led to the chapel corridor. The door stood open. She put her finger to her lips, then spoke in a barely audible voice. "We have to write down everything we say and give it to Mother Alphonsine every day."

"Why?" Melanie had taken a step closer in order to hear what the novice was saying.

"It's a way of keeping silence." Sister Geraldine kept her head bowed as she twirled the small pencil between her thumb and fingers.

"A way of keeping silence?"

Sister Geraldine took in a gulp of air and blew it out in a gust of impatience. "Well, you've been here three months by now. You know the rule of silence. We're not supposed to talk unless we have to. We're supposed to be recollected at all times. We're supposed to try and keep in union with God. We're not supposed to be going around saying any old thing, otherwise we'll break recollection and might fail in charity. You know all that. You shouldn't have asked me what this was."

Melanie said nothing, but kept staring at her, her lips parted.

"When you're a novice you have to write down everything you say, that's all. It's nothing. It's just a way of reminding us to keep silence." Sister Geraldine gave another impatient sigh, closed the booklet, fit the pencil against it and put it in her pocket. "Come on. We have to get those covers on before the bell rings." Her voice was now so soft that she was almost mouthing the words.

They headed out the sacristy door and into the sanctuary of the chapel, Melanie carrying the ladder and Sister Geraldine the armload of purple cloths. The faint light of late afternoon gave the chapel interior a subdued glow, making everything muted and indistinct. The kneeling black figures of two nuns appeared in the dimness toward the back of the long rows of wooden pews. The scent of beeswax clung to the air. In the sanctuary, the white-filigreed main altar stood out against the wooden backdrop. The red sanctuary light hung in its golden encasement from the central rafter. On the two side altars, the statues of Our Lady and St. Joseph appeared in soft shades of blue and brown, and in front of each shone the light from a vigil candle. The footsteps of the novice and postulant broke through the sanctuary's hush.

Sister Geraldine gestured to Melanie to put down the ladder at the side of Our Lady's altar. She peeled away one of the cloths, handed the remaining pile to Melanie and climbed the ladder. She gathered up the purple folds of the cloth and reached up to the blue-veiled head of the statue, then let go. The folds fell over the outstretched hands, covering the bare feet and the orange-tongued head of the snake beneath them, falling around the base like a limp parachute. Sister Geraldine smiled down at Melanie, a look of relief brightening her face.

They then climbed the three steps to the main altar, and Sister Geraldine set the ladder in front of the tabernacle. They genuflected, and Sister Geraldine picked among the folds and held up the smaller of the two remaining cloths. She gestured to Melanie to climb the ladder and then handed her the cloth. Melanie reached up to the crucifix above the tabernacle and slid the cloth over it. She looked down at Sister Geraldine. The novice nodded. "Okay," she said. Her voice reverberated through the silent sanctuary. Melanie looked down the length of the chapel, where the black figures of the nuns knelt motionless, and then back at Sister Geraldine.

The novice had already folded the ladder and was moving over to St. Joseph's altar. The brown-clad statue of the saint held a staff on which a lily sprouted. Sister Geraldine again mounted the ladder and Melanie handed her the remaining cloth. The two watched as the covering fell to midway down St. Joseph's garment. They stared at the statue's sandaled feet, and then Sister Geraldine said aloud, "Bloody hell." Melanie's eyes widened and she put her hand to her mouth and looked again down into the chapel. Neither of the black figures moved. Sister Geraldine heaved a sigh and said, in a whisper this time, "It's the damn lily. We'll have to change them around." She reached up and picked up the cloth from around the staff and lily, and then lifted the whole thing and handed the bundle down to Melanie. Just then they heard the sound of a handbell at the back of the chapel. It was the novice bell-ringer's announcement that time for charges was over. They had ten minutes to pull the ends of their work together, change into their regular habits and then hurry to the novices' common room for the evening reading.

They scurried across to Our Lady's altar, stopping to give a cursory genuflection in front of the tabernacle. With jerky movements, her face glistening with perspiration, Sister Geraldine pulled the cloth from Our Lady's statue, handed it down to Melanie and replaced it with the other cloth. They retraced their steps, half genuflecting this time, Sister Geraldine carrying the ladder in an awkward grasp. She took the final cloth, climbed the ladder and let it go over St. Joseph's statue. Then, without a backwards look, she pulled the ladder together and hurried out of the sanctuary. The two of them snapped up the mop, dusters and broom that stood together at the far door of the sacristy and made for the back staircase, then up to the linen room.

The small linen room was crowded with novices and postulants elbow to elbow in various stages of changing from their work clothes to their black habits. Dressed in sleeveless black and white checkered petticoats that covered long-sleeved undershirts, they jostled one another in silence as they moved back and forth between a long low bench and grey cupboards that lined two walls of the room. White undercaps hugged the novices' heads and fastened under their chins. Fringes of hair peeked out onto their foreheads and the napes of their necks. Sister Geraldine undid her veil, placed it on the bench and steered through the flurry of heavy black habits and shuffling bodies. "Excuse me, Sister," she murmured, making her way to her cupboard. Around her the other novices were attaching their rosaries to their belts, the beads clacking against each other. Lifting her habit over her head, she caught Melanie's eye. The two stared at each other, both faces flushed, their eyes expressionless.

As the five-minute bell struck, Sister Geraldine collided with another novice in the doorway of the common room. Still straightening her veil and attaching her rosary to her belt, she grabbed her black sewing bag from the back cupboard and sat down at the far end of the brown table that extended down the length of the room from the novice mistress's desk. Around her, others were opening their bags and spreading flowered dust cloths over their laps. Mother Alphonsine, the novice mistress, sat upright behind her desk at the top of the room, her back straight. She held a small piece of white lace, and her hand was already working the thread with a crochet hook. Her glasses sat on the bridge of her nose. On her desk lay a pile of stitched-up booklets like Sister Geraldine's, with greeting-card covers showing pictures of spring flowers and poinsettias, and, on one, a gold-embossed *Happy Birthday*.

At the end of the table, to Sister Geraldine's immediate right, sat Sister Lucy. A book lay open on the table in front of her. Her small face was white and pinched, and she ran her hand up and down the centre of the book in a nervous motion. Beneath dark eyebrows, her eyes darted from the book to the novice mistress and back again. Sister Geraldine gave a quick glance to the top of the table, pushed her chair slightly backwards until the novice mistress's line of vision was blocked by the bulky figure of the novice next to her, and pulled from her pocket the booklet of silence pages. She began to write, in a list, *It says Passion. Purple cloths. It must be there.* She massaged her bottom lip with her upper teeth and then continued. *We have to –*

"Praise be to Jesus," said Mother Alphonsine into the silence of the room, and Sister Lucy opened the book and made the sign of the cross. "In the name of the Father and of the Son and of the Holy Ghost." Around the room, everyone crossed herself. "A reading from *Christ the Life of the Soul*, 'Death to Sin' continued." She gave an anxious look toward the novice mistress.

"*Yes,* Sister," said Mother Alphonsine with a note of impatience.

Sister Lucy lowered her head toward the book. "'*If we want to know what God thinks of sin, let us look at Jesus in His Passion. When we behold God strike His Son, Whom He infinitely loves, with the death of the cross, we understand a little of what sin is in God's sight . . .* '"

Sister Geraldine placed her silence pages back in her pocket and, as the reading progressed, she emptied her bag and unwrapped her needlework from her dust cloth, which she spread over her lap.

AT RECREATION that evening one of the novices said, "Mother, doesn't the chapel look bleak now, with all the statues covered?"

The novices and postulants sat in a semicircle around the novice mistress's desk. The long table had been moved to the back of the room. Mother Alphonsine looked over her glasses, a needle in one hand and a piece of white thread in the other. Both were poised in the air, as she prepared to thread the needle. "Yes, we're moving into Passiontide, the most sombre time of the Lenten season. We're entering into the Passion of Our Lord, walking with him toward Golgotha. It's good for us to see an outward form of the inward state that we should be contemplating."

"St. Joseph's feet aren't covered, Mother. I could see them peeking out from under the purple cloth. The brown sandals and the pink toes," said Sister Pauline.

"And what was Sister contemplating looking at the sandal and the pink toes?" Sister Camillus winked over at her.

"Yes, the covering on St. Joseph's statue just needs to be straightened out. I'm sure Sister Geraldine will see to it before Mass tomorrow morning," said Mother Alphonsine.

Sister Geraldine kept her head lowered. She was working on a black stocking, the toe of it stretched over a darning mushroom.

"Is someone darning black on black at night?" Sister Geraldine looked up to see Mother Alphonsine's eyes upon her, her voice gently reproving. "We must preserve our eyes. We need our sight to labour in God's vineyard."

"I never realized before I entered how much of a strain it is to sew black on black in the artificial light, Mother," said the novice next to Sister Geraldine. "It's really a common sense rule, when you think about it."

Sister Geraldine reddened and with flustered hands pulled the darning mushroom out of the stocking and shoved both in her bag. In slow motion she pulled out a small piece of needlework. She yanked up an orange thread from the cloth and brought the needle down onto a half-finished poppy petal.

One of the novices was telling a joke. "Mudder, 'ow do you get beanut budder off the roof of your moud?" She was doing her best to keep her tongue touching the roof of her mouth to simulate something stuck there.

The others looked at the novice, eager and smiling. She attached her needle to the top of the cloth she was holding and reached up into her mouth with her index finger. "You can take your finger and ged id oud like this" – and she ran her finger along the inside of her mouth, then resumed a normal voice, holding her finger in the air. "Now you have peanut butter on your finger. How do you get it off? You can shake it off" – and she flung her finger downward – "or –" She paused and looked at her finger as if pondering hard. "– or you can put it in your mouth," and she put her finger back into her mouth and ran her top teeth along it. She looked around, deadpan. "Ow do you get beanut budder off the roof of your moud?"

Everyone laughed and several began to talk at once. "Mother –" "Mother, did you –" "Mother – ?"

Mother Alphonsine waved her hand and shook her head, still smiling. "One-at-a-time. Yes, Sister Geraldine."

"Oh, Mother, I didn't say anything," said Sister Geraldine, looking up.

"Did Sister Geraldine get the joke, Mother?" said one of the novices.

Sister Geraldine opened her lips and then closed them again, attempting a smile. Melanie piped up, "Sure she did, Mother, but I'll bet she was still thinking about St. Joseph's sandals."

Sister Geraldine shot her head down toward her needlework and pulled hard on the orange thread, then turned the cloth over and tried with the tip of her needle to untangle a mound of threads at the back.

Eventually the house bell sounded the end of recreation and Mother Alphonsine intoned, "Praise be to Jesus," and the novices and postulants gathered up their needlework into their dust cloths and pushed them into their bags. As the other novices were moving the chairs back and bringing the long table up to the centre of the room, Sister Geraldine watched Mother Alphonsine head for the door. She bumped her way past the others and followed the novice mistress.

"Mother," she called into the corridor, which by now was darkened.

Mother Alphonsine turned. Her eyes expressed surprise. She put her finger to her mouth.

*Silence Pages*

"Mother, may I speak to you please?"

"There isn't time, Sister, before night prayers, and after that of course it's the Great Silence. What is it? Can it not wait?"

"Mother, I didn't hand in my silence pages before the reading —"

"I noticed. I'll speak to you tomorrow." Mother Alphonsine turned toward the staircase. She cast a large shadow on the corridor wall.

"Mother —" Mother Alphonsine's silent figure was already halfway down the corridor.

At the silent examen after night prayers, Sister Geraldine pulled the booklet from her pocket and opened it to the page where she had written her list. Ahead, in the dim chapel light, all the altars were now devoid of flowers. The covered figures — Our Lady, St. Joseph and the crucifix — stood against the white altars like rocky outcrops. The sanctuary lamp that hung down from the ceiling in front of the tabernacle and the votive candles — yellow for St. Joseph, blue for Our Lady, a single one in front of each statue — were all that lit the sanctuary. The tiny lights made lively shadows on the dark figures.

She looked back down at the last entry in her booklet. *We have to —*

THE NEXT MORNING, as usual, the house bell roused the community at five-thirty. Their shoes padded along the polished corridors toward the chapel and at the entrance each one prayed in silence for a moment and then knelt, bent over and kissed the floor. At the meditation, a nun read from the back, a lamp behind her the only light in the chapel. "'*Contemplate Christ Jesus on His way to Calvary, laden with His Cross. He falls under the weight of this burden.*'"

Sister Geraldine knelt looking ahead at the sanctuary. The altars and the shrouded figures were becoming more distinct in the grey morning light. She sat down and once again pulled the booklet from her pocket. She opened it to the page from yesterday. *We have to –*

The reader broke in, "'*Eternal Father, look upon this altar, look upon Thy Son Who loved me and gave Himself for me on Calvary; forget those faults I have committed against Thy goodness. I offer Thee this oblation –*'"

Sister Geraldine closed her booklet and put it back in her pocket. She sat forward, expectant. After several minutes, the house bell announced that the priest had arrived for Mass: her cue to light the candles. She rose and, her head bowed and her white veil pulled forward over each shoulder as was the custom when the nuns were in chapel, she walked up the side aisle and opened the gate of the communion rail. She genuflected before the tabernacle and walked around the steps to the back of the altar. In the cramped, dark space, she fumbled around the tiny shelf. Taking in shallow breaths, she groped farther back. "Melanie, *where did you put them?*" she whispered into the stale air, her hands growing grimy from dust and the residue of candle wax. She hesitated, breathing anxiously, and then, head bowed, emerged back into the sanctuary. She walked with a mechanical stiffness toward the sacristy door.

Inside the sacristy, the priest looked up from the cupboard where the Mass vestments had been laid out. He had sandy-coloured hair and a cowlick at the back of his head. Stray hairs from his bushy eyebrows dipped down into his eyes. He was dressed in a black soutane, the white amice already criss-crossed over his chest, and he held the alb in bunched-up folds above his head, poised to let it drop. Beneath his soutane, his black shoes were scuffed and worn. He stopped at the sight of Sister Geraldine as if in a pantomime, his mouth half open.

"Father," Sister Geraldine's eyes blinked, lashless and quick, "Do you have any matches? There aren't any behind the altar. The only other thing I can do is get the ladder and bring down the sanctuary lamp and get a light from there. Mother Alphonsine will kill me if I do that, well she'll kill me anyway, but I need to have a light for the Mass candles."

The priest kept his eyes on her and, with a slow smile, brought the alb over his head and let its white folds rest around his shoulders. He reached into the pocket of his soutane and pulled out a silver lighter with the angular emblem of the Knights of Columbus and its jumble of symbols embossed in the centre. He held it toward her, but as Sister Geraldine reached for it, he pulled his hand back. His eyes were still on her face, and his lips turned upward at the corners. He held the lighter out to her again. She reached for it, more tentatively this time, and again he pulled it back. He laughed as he slipped his arms into the sleeves of the alb and let the garment fall to his shoes. The laugh, emanating from the back of his throat, sounded like a cackle. His fist around the lighter, he picked up the cincture that Sister Geraldine had arranged in the form of an M on top of the purple chasuble. "Caught you negligent, have I, Sister?" He was no longer looking at her.

Sister Geraldine's voice shook. "It's just that I had so much to do yesterday. I didn't know where the purple coverings were and I had to look all over the place for them, and then I used up the last match on the votive candles for night prayers last night. I didn't know — Mother Alphonsine is so —"

"I'm a former Boy Scout. I help old ladies across the street; I help damsels in distress. I've never been asked to help out a novice in trouble with her novice mistress."

He fumbled with the effort to tie the cincture around his waist and then opened his fist and threw the lighter in Sister Geraldine's direction. "Catch!"

Sister Geraldine bent and scooped it up from the priest's throw. "Thank you, Father." She flicked the lighter, but nothing happened. He looked up and cackled again, watching her. She tried it again, her hands shaking now, her lips tight, her face blotchy with embarrassment, and finally a small flame glowed.

"Voilà, Sister!" The priest reached for the purple chasuble.

"Thank you." Sister Geraldine's voice was a whisper, and she turned toward the door.

The chapel lights, no longer dimmed, now blazed. She went behind the altar, and, her hands still shaking, she reached for the brass extinguisher and then lifted the silver lighter to the taper attached to it. Her breathing still shallow, she walked around to the front of the altar, and as she put her foot on the first step to the high altar she stumbled on her skirt. The flame listed in front of her toward the carpet. She straightened, lifted her skirt and lit one Mass candle, and then, genuflecting in front of the tabernacle, the other.

Behind the altar again, she blew the flame out and proceeded back to the sacristy with the lighter. Inside, the priest, fully vested, stood ready for Mass. He gazed at her with expressionless eyes, held out his hand and took the lighter from her. He then followed her into the sanctuary. Her head bowed in humiliation, she made for the open gate of the communion rail. The nuns had risen as one body at the first sign of the priest's entrance.

"Sister Geraldine, I'll speak to you now, please." Mother Alphonsine had risen from her place at the head of the horseshoe-shaped table in the novices' cramped refectory, and the novices and postulants, crowded around the table, stood up and pushed their stools under the table as she walked out, her habit and rosary beads brushing against the wall.

"Mother." Sister Geraldine looked down at the remains of an orange still on her plate and the milky coffee in her cup, and then up at Mother Alphonsine.

The novice mistress waved her hand. "You can finish that later." Sister Geraldine squeezed past the others, past the sideboard where the porridge dishes had been placed, and followed Mother Alphonsine into the corridor.

When they reached the passageway leading to the back entrance, Mother Alphonsine drew her aside. Outside, three concrete steps led up to the ground level. A strong wind was blowing the branches of a tree against the windows. A nun stepped past them, a black shawl bundled around her shoulders. As she opened the door, a blast of wind swept into the passageway. Sister Geraldine shivered as she faced Mother Alphonsine, her hands clasped in front of her.

"What happened this morning, Sister?"

Sister Geraldine looked the novice mistress briefly in the eye and then brought her gaze down to the baseboard along the wall. "Mother, I'm sorry. We ran out of matches. I'm sorry, Mother. May I make reparation?"

"You know there is to be no contact with the priest in the sacristy. You know this. You should have spoken to me."

"Yes, Mother." Sister Geraldine continued looking at the baseboard.

"I won't ask for a rendering right now, but you will of course include it in your silence pages. And by the way, I did not receive your silence pages yesterday."

"I know, Mother. It's just that I had to speak to Melanie about those coverings on the statues, and we had a hard time finding them, and then, when we got them on, we had the wrong cloths on Our Lady and St. Joseph. St. Joseph had to have the bigger one. I thought it didn't matter which cloth went where, except for the crucifix. I knew it would be the smallest cloth. But we had to put the biggest cloth on St. Joseph because of the lily sticking out of his stick. Or I mean his staff." She curved her fingers into a loose fist and pumped up and down with her arm to signify the statue's position. "And we didn't have much time because it took so long to find the cloths, and then we had to change them around because the smaller cloth came down only halfway on St. Joseph and you could see the bottom of the statue and his feet, and we had to –" She breathed in sharply and put her hand to her mouth, and her face crumpled into sobs.

"That's fine, Sister." Mother Alphonsine's voice was gentle. "We'll discuss it later. In the meantime, yes, you may make reparation before this morning's instruction."

"Thank you, Mother."

Later, in the sacristy, wearing a blue apron over her habit, Sister Geraldine began putting away the Mass vestments. They were, as usual, left in the same order in which they had been laid out, but less carefully. The cincture had been tossed to one side, the tassles dangling down in front of the cupboard. The alb had been flung inside out, the arms askew, over top of the chasuble. A smell of male perspiration and tobacco smoke pervaded the area around the discarded vestments.

Together, Sister Geraldine and Melanie cleared the altar of the Mass articles: the water and wine cruets in their glass tray, the hand cloth, the large red missal in its wooden stand. Then together they placed the green felt cloth, with the gold-embroidered words, "Jesus My Lord My God My All," over the altar. Back in the sacristy, the two of them stood before the table on which the priest had placed the purple veil covering the chalice. Sister Geraldine held up a pair of white gloves and handed them to Melanie, then motioned for her to put the gloves on.

As Melanie donned the gloves, she looked over toward the door to the chapel corridor and whispered, "Why did Mother speak to you after breakfast? What did she want?" She removed the veil from the chalice and handed it to Sister Geraldine, who pulled out a long drawer and laid it flat inside. Beneath it, the colours of other veils peeped out – green, red, gold, white, and at the bottom, black. When she turned back to the table she saw that Melanie was watching her. She shook her head and put her finger to her lips.

"What did she want?" Melanie removed the white purificator and the burse from the chalice and paten. The gold vessels gleamed against the dark brown of the table. "Did you do something wrong?"

"Everything. I did everything wrong." The novice stood aside as Melanie picked up the chalice and paten and took them to the piscine and turned on the tap. Several days earlier, giving Melanie the tour of the sacristy, Sister Geraldine had said, "This is a piscine." Melanie had put her hand to her mouth to suppress a laugh. "Piss-ine?" she said. Sister Geraldine had carried on with great earnestness, "It doesn't connect to the normal drains. It goes straight to the ground. This is used to wash out the chalice and the paten. It's because they have held the body and blood of Christ." Now she stood tight-lipped.

"What did you do wrong?" Melanie raised her voice slightly over the sound of the running water. "We got the coverings on the statues all right, didn't we? So the cloth didn't cover St. Joseph's foot. So what. Big deal."

"She didn't say anything about St. Joseph's foot. It was more important things. Matters of obedience. Obedience is serious."

"What did you do that was against obedience?" Melanie had turned off the tap and was drying the chalice with a cloth.

"Not having permission to do things and doing them anyway. Going into the sacristy without permission when the priest was there. Talking when I shouldn't be."

"How come you had to go into the sacristy?"

"Matches." From a broom closet Sister Geraldine took out two mops and two dusters.

Melanie turned toward her and gasped. "I was supposed to get matches from Mother, wasn't I?"

Sister Geraldine nodded and handed her a broom and duster.

"Oh my gosh, I'm sorry. I forgot. It's just that there's so much to have to think about, there's so much to remember. What can I . . . ?"

Sister Geraldine waved her toward the door leading to the sanctuary. "Just – shut – up." She pressed her lips together.

When the door closed behind the postulant, Sister Geraldine ran the mop around the sacristy, beginning at the sanctuary door, then under the piscine, under the table, along the wall cupboard, the radiator and the priest's prie-dieu, and under the chair. She took the duster and ruffled it along the window ledges, the kneeler and the top of the prie-dieu, lifting the purple stole that was draped over it, and along the rungs and over the leather seat of the chair.

Leaning the mop on the table, she tiptoed over to the door, opened it quietly and looked into the sanctuary. Melanie's mop rested against the far wall and she was dusting the curlicues of the communion rail, her back to the door. Sister Geraldine let out a long, silent breath. She tiptoed back and sat down on the priest's chair, working her way to the edge of it, her back straight. She pulled her booklet from her pocket, took up the small pencil and opened the pages to the notations of the day before. *We have to –*

She looked toward the cupboard, now bare of vestments, and began to write. *Father, do you have matches?* She looked up again, swallowed, looked toward the window, then swung back to the stitched pages on her lap. She put her pencil down and rubbed her hands together. Her knuckles were chapped and red. She picked up the booklet and pencil again and continued writing. *There aren't any,* she wrote. *Thank you, Father.*

She stood up, ran her hand around the leather to smooth out any indication that she had sat on the priest's chair and was picking up the duster again just as Melanie came back into the sacristy.

# Mother and All Her Chicks

THE LONG WOODEN TABLE IN FRONT OF THE kitchen stove had been scrubbed clean and the wire basket sat in the middle of it, filled to the brim with eggs, their rounded tops smooth and pinky-white. Sister Geraldine loved the look of them there. An egg in an egg cup was boring to look at and boring to eat (though she'd never have said such a thing out loud), but piled up like this, almost overflowing the basket, the eggs seemed to glow with some inner light. The bounty of God's creation. An "apt symbol," Mother Alphonsine had said at last evening's recreation.

"Don't think the Easter egg is a purely secular invention," the novice mistress had said from behind her desk, folding and unfolding her hands. At Sunday recreation the novices' common room was bare of the usual busyness of needles and thread and bunches of cloth, and the novices sat in a half moon on plain wooden chairs with their hands on their black laps, their white-veiled heads sometimes turned to each other, but mostly facing Mother Alphonsine. "It is an apt symbol of the Resurrection. The new creation made manifest. Think of how a chicken bursts from the egg."

"But then the chicken is the better symbol of Easter, Mother," said one of the novices.

"What Mother is saying is that there is a miracle in the egg — something coming to life inside an inanimate object," said another. "Is that it, Mother?"

"Wasn't a fish the symbol of the early Christians, Mother?" This was Sister Mary Alma, who always threw a wrench into the subjects at recreation, and then looked around and grinned. "Why then didn't we have chocolate fish for tea today?"

"Well, the egg is also an ancient symbol of perfection." Mother Alphonsine seemed unwilling to let the subject go.

"Wasn't it the circle? Wasn't the circle the symbol of perfection and infinity?" asked someone at the far end of the row.

"With the egg, with the bursting of the chicken through the shell, you have the notion of Christ bursting through the bonds of death and sin, and poof! rolling the stone away, and appearing, alive, in all His infinite glory." The novice mistress was now speaking in a pontifical manner, intended, Sister Geraldine thought, not to brook any disagreement or the wrinkles that questioning might introduce.

But it didn't matter. The eggs had appeared on

their plates in the refectory for Easter Sunday's tea. The basement refectory, normally drab and plain, had been cheered and lightened with the appearance of multicoloured, foil-wrapped candies on the white plates at each person's place. Chocolate eggs. By evening, the novices and postulants were giddy with the feast day celebrations: the special meals, the extra recreation, the afternoon sleep they had been allowed because of the lateness of the midnight vigil the night before.

Then this morning, Easter Monday, Mother Alphonsine had taken Sister Geraldine aside after breakfast and said, "Don't change into your work clothes this morning. Stay in your black habit." She had hurried off, without further explanation. Sister Geraldine went to her charge in the sacristy as usual, and as she was putting away the Mass vestments, Mother Alphonsine rushed into the sacristy, her black veil flying so that the top of her fichu showed, revealing a small glimpse of her neck. "A surplice for Monsignor," she said, almost out of breath. "And the aspergillum and stoup."

"The what, Mother?" Sister Geraldine was conscious of backing away, recoiling from the placid novice mistress, who had suddenly become frenzied and flustered.

"A surplice. Any one will do. And the aspergillum and stoup." She still seemed to be rushing, her body tense and shaking. "Hurry, Sister!"

Sister Geraldine withdrew from the sacristy closet a white surplice on a hanger. Mother Alphonsine grabbed it and was removing it from the hanger when Monsignor appeared – or, as Sister Geraldine immediately perceived it, he filled the doorway. He was short and stout, and he strutted into the sacristy, the magenta band around the wide girth of his stomach preceding him like an advance guard.

"Oh, Monsignor –" Mother Alphonsine's voice had changed to a coo, and splotches of red appeared on her cheeks. She held out the surplice to him and as he put it on over his head, she made a motion to Sister Geraldine.

Sister Geraldine stared at her, her mouth opening and closing, overcome with a feeling of misery and helplessness.

The novice mistress gave a sigh of exasperation and brushed past her, her face now flaming. She opened one of the cupboards and pulled out the brass asperges vessel and the cylindrical tube whose name Sister Geraldine had never learned and so always thought of as "the holy water blessing thing." Sister Geraldine sprang to another cupboard where a large jar contained holy water. She unscrewed the lid and poured water into the vessel, which Mother Alphonsine held with shaking hands.

"It's the Easter blessing," the novice mistress whispered. "I'll take Monsignor around and you'll follow with the stoup."

Monsignor was fumbling with the pages of a small black book and mumbling in Latin, "'*Asperges me hysopo et mundabor, lavabo me et super nivem dealbabor.*'" Sister Geraldine recognized *hysopo* and *lavabo* from the psalm that they had recited after night prayers during Lent: *Thou shalt sprinkle me with hyssop and I shall be cleansed; Thou shalt wash me and I shall be made whiter than snow.*

AND NOW Sister Geraldine beheld the eggs on the kitchen table. Beside them lay a basket full of the special Easter buns that Sister Cook had baked on Holy Saturday, the aroma of which had filled the back staircase all day. They had been brushed with milk before baking, and they glistened and glowed, yeasty and full and light.

The kitchen, always alive with Sister Cook's darting here and there, stood empty, as if it were on display as a museum piece. Sister Geraldine knew Sister Cook was probably hiding in the pantry across the hall, rubbing her arthritic hands together and perhaps muttering Hail Marys, trying vainly to keep impatience in check. The procession had made its way toward the kitchen, Mother Alphonsine's bobbing head and twitching veil leading the way, Monsignor waddling behind with his head down and she herself taking up the rear with the aspergillum and stoup. As they came near, Sister Geraldine saw another novice, Sister Lucy, dressed in her white broadcloth work habit, the sleeves rolled to her elbows, darting across the corridor to the pantry, a tub of vegetables in her short arms. By the time they reached the kitchen, the pantry door was closed, with not a sound on the other side of it.

Monsignor, short and squat in his purple-piped cassock and white surplice, mumbled a string of Latin words from the black prayer book in his hands as the three stood before the eggs and buns. Sparse white hair clung to the soft pink of his skull. He reached toward Sister Geraldine and grasped the aspergillum. He shook it over the table and Sister Geraldine watched as the drops fell.

As he replaced it, Mother Alphonsine bowed to him, her black veil falling over her shoulders and nearly covering her face, and then she led the way out of the kitchen toward the nuns' refectory. Behind her, limping or perhaps only plodding in the manner of old people, Monsignor appeared several inches shorter than the novice mistress.

He stopped suddenly and did a half turn toward Sister Geraldine. A pale blue eye peered at her over rimless glasses beneath a thick white eyebrow. "Are you the Donleavy girl?" His voice was growly, not unkind, but with the air of one who is used to commanding respect.

Sister Geraldine stopped short and gave a slight gasp at the suddenness of his attention. "No, Monsignor." She swallowed the words and wondered if he had heard her.

"Oh. Then who are you?" He looked at her full-face this time. One of his eyelids drooped. His face was pink like his skull, with fine filigreed veins along his cheeks.

Sister Geraldine hesitated and looked ahead at Mother Alphonsine, who had turned toward them.

"Sister Geraldine," she said. "Monsignor," she added. Sister Geraldine swallowed, confused, and felt her face reddening.

"Well, what's your last name?" Frown lines appeared in the soft flesh above his nose.

She looked again at the novice mistress. "Moran," she answered.

Mother Alphonsine gave a short, forced laugh, halfway between a chuckle and a groan. "She's not from Purification parish, Monsignor," she said.

"Oh. Well, we won't hold that against you." The frown lines disappeared, but the face remained bland and fleshy and pink. There was no hint of a smile.

SISTER GERALDINE couldn't remember Monsignor's last name, although she must have heard it at one time. She knew him only from St. Monica's Thursday afternoon Confessions before each month's First Fridays. "Confession afternoons," the girls called them. For the whole afternoon the classes took turns walking in lines from St. Monica's, the high school across the garden, to Purification Church for Confession before First Friday Mass. (The Mass began at nine o'clock on First Friday mornings, and that meant school didn't start until ten, a tradition that had given rise to the church's nickname: "Pure Vacation.") The first thing to be seen inside the church's dark interior was the oversized crucifix with its graphic blood and nails, which hung over the altar, in relief against the yellow frosted sanctuary windows.

Monsignor's confessional was the one closest to the back of the church on the left side, the side where the statue of St. Rita stood, dressed not dissimilarly from the nuns at St. Monica's, with the fake blood appearing just below her white bandeau. The blood emanated from the place where a thorn pierced her forehead, Sister Geraldine had learned from her *Child's Book of Saints,* a thorn that Jesus Himself had given her.

Sister Geraldine, in thinking back to the Thursday confessions, always associated the dusty statue of St. Rita with Monsignor's confessional. The girls all lined up at the right side of the church, near the confessional of one of the other priests. Those priests tended to be young, some of them handsome, and somewhat shy in confession. Everyone avoided Monsignor's confessional because, it was said, he spoke aloud instead of whispering, and had once shouted, "What? Speak up, girl, speak up! I can't hear what you're saying!" The other girls had to cover their ears, because it was at least a venial sin, and probably a mortal one, to listen deliberately to another's confession.

One day, when the right side of the church was filled and no one knelt on the left side, Sister Barbara came up to her – she was still Gerry then, of course – and poked her in the arm and gestured her toward Monsignor's confessional. With a feeling of black dread, she moved aside the heavy wine-coloured curtain and entered the dark space. She groped for the kneeler and knelt down, trying to fit the skirt of her uniform under her knees to mitigate the hardness of the kneeler. At the same time she felt a keen need to urinate. She tightened her buttocks and the muscles on the insides of her thighs. Then a voice boomed in her face, "All right, what is it?" and she imagined its echo throughout the whole vast church, and the throng of girls turning as one body toward Monsignor's confessional, waiting for her to come out. Her eyes had become accustomed to the dark interior and she could see the outline of Monsignor's profile against the screened opening and could smell old-man perspiration.

Something propelled her at that moment to get up off her knees and sweep aside the heavy confessional curtain, and as she heard Monsignor's voice, gruff and uncomprehending, "Go on! What is it?" from inside his box, she made her way past the girls kneeling at the back of the church, who turned their heads to stare at her. She found the women's washroom in the church hall and stood by the outside door counting the nails in the door frame until she saw the familiar faces of her class emerging from the church along the sidewalk, the scarves still on their heads. "Where have you been?" one of them asked as she slipped into line with them.

"Helping Sister," she mumbled, looking at the ground, trying to appear purposeful.

"Helping her with what?"

"Helping her with – help." She tried to give her voice a tone of mystery and importance, but felt silly and exposed.

"What did Monsignor say?" asked a voice behind her.

She kept on walking, face to the front. "He said to say three Hail Marys." She hadn't gone to Confession, and in the space of a minute now she had just told three lies. She wanted a huge road roller to come crashing along the street and crush them all into bits, herself and her deceiving tongue among them.

But her sense of guilt didn't last long; she survived the inquisition from the other girls, and best of all, Sister Barbara, who had eyes on every side of her head, was never the wiser. And now she was walking behind Monsignor inside the cloister of all places, looking at the white hairs on his pink neck and the Roman collar sticking up from his black soutane, yellowy brown at the top edge that came in contact with his skin. And here she was, in the very same habit of the Order that Sister Barbara and all the rest of the nuns wore, except for the white veil that marked her as a novice.

At the door of the nuns' refectory, Mother Alphonsine stood aside for Monsignor to enter. She and Sister Geraldine followed. In the refectory, a horseshoe-shaped table stood covered with oilcloth, white napkins wrapped around cutlery at each place. Wooden chairs were set in against the table. Monsignor opened his prayer book and mumbled some Latin, then reached for the aspergillum as he had done in the kitchen. After the blessing, the novice mistress led the way out of the room and into the novices' refectory across the hall.

This room was a tiny replica of the nuns' refectory: a horseshoe table that filled nearly the whole space, napkins wrapped around cutlery. The novice mistress's chair stood at the top of the room, and under the table, the novices' stools. A black crucifix hung on the wall. On the sideboard sat a thick green book that was being read during meals while everyone ate in silence. Monsignor set down his own prayer book and picked up the green book, turning it sideways to look at the title on the spine. "*Father William Doyle,*" he read. "Who's he?"

"Oh, he was a Jesuit, Monsignor." Mother Alphonsine had become flustered again and a red spot appeared on each cheek. "A very holy man. He was killed on the battlefield in France during the First World War and is believed to have died in the odour of sanctity. He is considered a martyr. His – I believe his cause for beatification has been introduced."

"His cause for beatification has been introduced. Oh, well. His cause has been introduced." He cleared his throat and put the book down and picked up his prayer book again. Then he spoke in a high, girlish voice, "He died in the odour of sanctity and his cause has been introduced. And oh, a Jesuit!" His shaggy white eyebrows rose and fell, and he looked at Sister Geraldine with watery eyes and lifted one corner of his mouth into a partial smile.

The novice mistress massaged the white knuckles of her left hand with her right thumb. Red patches now covered her face, and on the side of her nose, a pimple that never seemed to heal had turned purple and orange. Her veil and wimple were frozen into position. The straight line of her mouth turned inward as Monsignor repeated the blessing ritual and shook the holy water over the tiny room. As he turned toward Sister Geraldine to replace the aspergillum, Mother Alphonsine reached over for the stoup. "I'll take that now, Sister," she said. "There's no need for you to come along anymore." Her voice dripped ice water. "This way now, Monsignor."

Monsignor bowed his head, looking like a scolded schoolchild with his tender pink scalp and sparse strands of white hair, and followed her out the door in a thick blend of white and black, his magenta sash sliding along the door frame.

Sister Geraldine stood listening to the quiet tread of their feet down the corridor. Within seconds, there was no sound except the brush of a twig outside against the window in the early spring wind. She stared around at the white oilcloth of the table, the small brown cupboard that held the novices' dishes and the thick green book lying askew on the sideboard where Monsignor had put it down. For the first time since she had entered the convent, apart from a few hours on Sunday afternoons, she was at loose ends, her minutes not filled with a task that had been dictated by holy obedience. What time was it, anyway? She looked down to see that the forefinger of her right hand was drawing a circle on the table, starting from a centre point and moving farther and farther out. A trickle of watery mucus was making its way down her nasal canal. She sniffed it back and abruptly pulled a large white handkerchief from her pocket and dabbed her nose. She tiptoed to the door, which had been left ajar at the departure of Mother Alphonsine and Monsignor, and quietly closed it. She picked up the book, pulled one of the stools from underneath the table and sat down, crossing her legs.

This biography of Father Doyle was difficult to listen to in the refectory while they ate their potatoes and beef stew and apple cake. He was a priest who was given to severe penances – hair shirts, and wires around his legs and waist that cut into his flesh. He shunned all comforts, sleeping on the floor, going on and on in his diary about refusing to take sugar in his tea and trying to eat without enjoying his food.

The book opened at the place where yesterday's reading had finished. She fingered the smooth surface of the bookmark with her thumb. The bookmark was a plastic-covered holy card showing the Shroud of Jesus and His face imprinted on it. It looked like the negative of a photograph, Jesus's features white against a brown background. A thick moustache ran between an elongated nose and a narrow mouth. His hair and the marks sloping downwards on his forehead looked like pieces of straw. Sister Geraldine supposed that the forehead marks had been made by the crown of thorns. The picture made her shudder with the feeling that she was looking into an exhumed coffin.

She looked down at the page that had fallen open. *During a mission I walked one night barefooted over the stones two miles to the chapel. I brought a razor with me, for I was longing to shed my blood for Jesus, as His victim. Kneeling at the altar, I made a deep gash on my breast.* And further on: *Several times I have undressed and rolled in furze bushes. The pain of the thousands of little pricks is intense for days afterwards. Once or twice I have forced my way through a thorn hedge, which tore and wounded me frightfully – for Jesus' love.* She felt as if a weight were pushing against her chest, as if a bulldozer were bearing down on her. Her lips were pieces of rubber, and the bandeau across her forehead and the tight casing of her wimple pushed inward so that her head felt like a crush of broken skull. The book, heavy in her hands, pulled her downward.

She replaced the bookmark with its shroud of Jesus, placed the book on the table and looked up at the window. In spite of the blustery wind, the sun was shining, and the slender shadow of a bush and the glint of the rays on a dusty remnant of snow seemed to lift the weight somewhat.

She looked back down at the book. Why didn't she seek to do extra penances for the love of Jesus? Why didn't she ask Mother Alphonsine if she might sleep on the floor, if she might take only bread and water for a day? If she might roll in a bunch of bushes? She smiled at the thought of Mother Alphonsine's face if she asked to go jumping around naked inside a thicket of brambles. Still, why did the novice mistress have this book read in the refectory if the novices were not somehow to be edified by the saintly priest, and in some way use him as a model for their religious lives?

At the very least, she could try to love the Thursday Holy Hour, which the community spent in silence after night prayers. She knew the origin of the practice –"Could you not spend one hour with me?" Jesus had said to His apostles the Thursday night before He died – but she couldn't help it; she hated the Holy Hour. It was boring to look at the tabernacle and try to pray when the novices already spent five hours a day in the chapel. What more was there to say to God?

She had once taken with her to the Holy Hour a book of prayers from the common room cupboard, hoping that it might help her to pass the time. But the frontispiece of the book featured a picture of Jesus behind prison bars, dressed in his stations-of-the-cross robes, with the crown of thorns on His head, the whole scene placed inside an altar tabernacle. Beneath the picture were the words, *Behold how Our blessed Saviour sits imprisoned, awaiting our love.* It had a similar effect on her to Father Doyle's life – a feeling of being in a crumbling, dank place where constrictions of every kind pressed her down, where the walls screeched at her of her own mediocrity, where her head was pressed into her chest and then jerked in every direction and weird creatures with wings and tails flew about, jeering at her state of worthlessness. It was the feeling that no matter what she did, no matter how many prayers she said during the Holy Hour, no matter how fervent she became, no matter how many penances she performed, nothing would make things right. Father Doyle loved the Holy Hour, and urged the practice of staying up on Thursday nights to pray. In fact, Father Doyle not only loved the Holy Hour, he prayed it lying prostrate on the ground, stretching his arms out as far as he could reach so that he might experience the most pain and discomfort possible. She remembered Monsignor's fleshy, mocking face and smiled. *Oh, a Jesuit!*

She looked down at the book and opened it at random. There he sat in a glossy photograph, dressed in a soldier's uniform, wearing the thick Roman collar of the military chaplain. He had big ears and a long nose and slicked-down hair. She turned more pages. *I arrived at the convent late in the evening . . .* He was writing from somewhere in France. War was going on. He was seeking accommodation from some nuns. *Mother and all her chicks came swarming in . . .*

The refectory door opened and Sister Lucy walked in, then stepped backwards and gasped when she saw Sister Geraldine. She carried a pitcher of water. Her small, peaked face blushed and her eyes widened beneath black eyebrows. For an instant it seemed as if the weight of the pitcher might overcome her.

Sister Geraldine uncrossed her legs, stood up immediately, and in one movement pushed the stool under the table and placed the book back on the sideboard. She then kept her hand on it, trying to appear nonchalant, but she knew that the anxiety rising within her made her movements appear furtive and sneaky. Would Sister Lucy tell Mother Alphonsine that she had come upon her sitting on a refectory stool with her legs crossed, reading a book? After all, a sister was supposed to tell the superior if she suspected another sister of doing something that was against the Holy Rule. Sitting and reading in the refectory was never even contemplated, let alone allowed. She knew, really, that even though Mother Alphonsine had not said as much, she should have left the refectory immediately. In fact, she knew that the novice mistress, if she hadn't been so flustered by Monsignor's comments, would have told her to return to her sacristy duties.

So she had done wrong, and Sister Lucy surely knew it. But nothing could rectify matters now. She would have to wait until Mother Alphonsine beckoned her aside after the visit to chapel – or unless she herself told the novice mistress what she had done, a scenario that she knew, as soon as it entered her consciousness, would never happen.

Sister Lucy mumbled, "Excuse me, Sister," and set the pitcher on the table. Sister Geraldine, feeling like a useless black blob, watched as the smaller novice skittered toward the cupboard, moving more freely in her white work habit with its short cape that allowed her arms freedom.

Sister Geraldine began trying to help – doing so would at least salvage some small part of her tattered character. She opened the overhead cupboard door and brought down the glasses. As she placed them on the table, Sister Lucy counted them, her lips moving with great earnestness, and then she poured water into them. When she had finished, she stood to one side, and Sister Geraldine was aware that they were both avoiding eye contact. Sister Lucy seemed not to know what to do with her hands once she put down the pitcher. She cupped one in the other, caressing it with her thumb, and then, as if her hands could not be trusted to remain in one position on their own, she clasped them together in front of her in an attitude of prayer.

The soft tinkle of the novice timekeeper's bell sounded in the distance, and the novices and postulants would soon be appearing from all over the convent for the ten o'clock drink of water. Sister Geraldine felt an almost tangible sense of relief emanating from the other novice. She leaned over and picked up a glass of water and, facing ahead, toward the crucifix on the wall, began to drink. She tried to blot Sister Lucy out of her field of vision, but it was impossible. For one thing, the room was too small, and for another, Sister Lucy leaned in front of her and, before drinking, made a sign of the cross. The sign of the cross! She was saying grace! Of course! Why had she herself forgotten it? This was the ritual they carried out day after day before the ten o'clock drink of water as well as before every meal. The most elementary prayer in the whole Catholic Church – grace before meals – and Sister Geraldine had forgotten it this morning. Was a blatant lapse like this the kind of thing that happened when one let obedience slide? That of course was what she had done. Instead of going back to her charge as she should have, she had stayed in the refectory. Sat down and crossed her legs, a failure in religious decorum. Read a book that wasn't even allowed to be read, except out loud at meals. As if it were Sunday afternoon. And now – forgetting to say grace before drinking her water.

"Today and tomorrow are double first-class feasts," Mother Alphonsine said when recreation got started that afternoon. "The joy of the Resurrection continues." She had regained her equilibrium, her face having resumed its usual yellowish pallor. Sister Geraldine had returned to the sacristy after the ten o'clock drink and was drying the cruets, her head bent over the towel, when Mother Alphonsine and Monsignor returned. Monsignor gave a grunt of exertion, followed by laboured breathing. Sister Geraldine kept her head bowed and turned away in an effort to look recollected. When they had left, she saw the white surplice on the table, one sleeve drooping toward the floor, and beside it the stoup with the aspergillum inside.

A few minutes later, as she was arranging the surplice on its hanger, she looked up to see Mother Alphonsine standing alone in the doorway. The novice mistress was holding her large rosary in both hands, fingering one bead after another. Her face was flushed. "Monsignor isn't well. You mustn't take notice of the things he said."

Sister Geraldine caught her breath. "Yes, Mother," she murmured.

Mother Alphonsine turned to leave, and then turned back. "Father Doyle *was* a holy man," she said. Her lower lip was quivering.

But now, the novice mistress was as chirpy as if she had just come with Mary Magdalene from the empty tomb. She pulled on her crochet thread and looked around with a smile. "Chocolates at tea today."

There was a general murmur around the group of novices and postulants. Sister Lucy sat up straight, looking downward, as if she hadn't been paying attention, or perhaps had other thoughts on her mind. Sister Geraldine opened her black work bag feeling disgruntled for reasons she couldn't explain to herself.

LATER, AT TEA, there they sat on the refectory table: three gold-covered chocolates on every plate. As refectorian, Sister Lucy stood at the end of the table closest to the sideboard, and Sister Geraldine sat on the inside, squeezed up directly opposite the novice mistress. She could feel, rather than see, Sister Lucy pouring the tea and passing the heavy white cups and saucers down the table. No reading took place at tea time, and the only sounds, after Sister Lucy had taken her seat at the end of the table, were the low rustle of shifting bodies as baskets of bread and dishes of butter were passed down each side, and then the clink of knives as the bread was cut and buttered. The added sounds today were the crackle of the gold wrapping as it came off the chocolates and then the clatter of knives breaking through them. Some of the knives made hardly discernible sounds, as when cutting through a chocolate with a cream filling, while others, especially if encountering a nut or toffee filling, came down with a crack that seemed nearly to break the plate. And then the sound of munching: all around the table, each slice of bread had been broken into six pieces and the chocolates had been cut equally, so that there was a bit of chocolate for each piece of bread.

Sister Geraldine had intended to look down the table at Sister Lucy's plate to see if there was chocolate on it. During the afternoon she had realized that the other novice struck her as an overly scrupulous goody-goody, someone who would seriously try to emulate Father William Doyle and who would probably ask to forego chocolates as a penance. But she didn't look down the table to see whether Sister Lucy was eating chocolates or not. She was too busy concentrating on her own chocolates, cutting them up and fitting them on her pieces of bread. It was, of course, something she would not ever have done before entering the convent; she would never have thought of cutting up a chocolate with a knife, or of eating chocolates with bread and butter. But, of course, before entering the convent, she could have eaten as many chocolates as she wanted. Now she could have only three. And she discovered that the richness and sweetness of the chocolate blended nicely with the plainness of the bread and butter.

Afterwards, she thought that perhaps she had deliberately avoided looking over at Sister Lucy during tea, that practising custody of the eyes in this way was a small penance she had imposed upon herself. But she wasn't sure.

# *Particular Friendship*

"Mother, does anyone remember the movie about a nun stranded on a tropical island?" asked one of the novices, adjusting her chair and looking up at the overhanging leaves of the giant weeping willow.

She looked around at the other ten novices and four postulants, and then at Mother Alphonsine, the novice mistress. They sat in a circle on the riverbank, their wooden chairs listing somewhat on the uneven ground. To one side of them, a branch of the weeping willow hung so low over the river that the outermost leaves almost touched the water.

They were all dressed in black – the postulants in black dresses and capes with black nets over their hair, and the novices like Mother Alphonsine, in the full nun's habit: white starched linen framing their faces, white bands across their foreheads and a long shapeless habit with a rosary hanging at the side. The only difference was that Mother Alphonsine wore a black veil and the novices' veils were white.

When she received no response to her question, the novice continued: "The nun was in the middle of the island, sweeping a grass hut, dressed in her full habit."

"What happened to her?" asked Mother Alphonsine, setting a soft black bag upon her lap.

"I don't quite remember, Mother. I think she might have been in a shipwreck or something. But her habit was perfectly pressed. And then who comes along? Who would you guess?"

"A priest?" ventured someone.

The novice shook her head.

"Mother Superior?" said another, laughing.

The novice shook her head again. "Uh-uh." She looked around the group. "Robert Mitchum. He's a movie star, Mother. He played a navy officer or something. But don't worry. At the end of the movie, Sister Whatever-her-name-is decides she's going to remain a nun and not marry him. They're rescued in the end of course."

"Why can't they leave nuns be?" said Mother Alphonsine. With a quick movement, she turned her bag upside down, and onto her lap fell a soft bundle in a flowered dust cloth. She unwrapped the bundle, and a piece of linen and cascading skeins of embroidery thread came loose. She laid the dust cloth across her lap and picked up the embroidery piece. Around the circle, the novices and postulants emptied bags of needlework similar to Mother Alphonsine's onto their laps.

"I read a book about a nun last year, Mother," said Annette, one of the postulants. "She lived in Belgium and went to Africa as a missionary, and then she came back to the convent in Belgium because she was sick. They're making a movie of it, and Audrey Hepburn's playing the nun. I read about it in a movie magazine." She clapped her hand over her mouth. "Oops, I'm sorry, Mother, I forgot we're not supposed to talk about those things."

"Six months you've been here, Annette?" said Mother Alphonsine, looking over the top of wire-rimmed glasses. "But never mind. As St. Paul says, the old man is still alive and it takes some time to root him out."

"Well, anyway, Mother, she decided to leave the convent. She wanted to give herself to God, but first of all she was more interested in fighting the Nazis, and so she left to join the Resistance. You can't just do that, can you, Mother — just go ahead and leave after you've made final vows?"

"I heard about that book," said Mother Alphonsine. "She said she didn't know if she could keep the religious vows, but that she'd try. *Try?!* That's not how it's done in the real world of religious life. You don't say you'll *try* to keep the vows, you say you *will*."

"What's the name of that book?" whispered Annette to Melanie, the postulant sitting next to her.

"*The Nun's Story,*" Melanie whispered back.

"Oh, that's right." Annette sat slouched on the edge of her chair, her knees drawn up, one foot crossed over the other. She faced Melanie and opened her mouth to say more.

"Did I say it's been six months?" Mother Alphonsine broke in, looking over at the two postulants. A gold tooth flashed in her mouth. The postulants drew back, their faces down. Annette straightened and slid her feet together. Around the group, a general rustle sounded as the others did likewise.

"Today's feast always makes me realize that summer is truly here," the novice mistress continued. She pulled up a thread out of a skein of blue embroidery cotton, and from her pocket withdrew a pair of scissors. "The Visitation – Mary goes to visit her cousin Elizabeth. Both women are carrying a child, a secret, hidden thing." She snipped the thread and smiled, her eyes crinkling as she peered over her glasses, the starched linen around her face stretching slightly. "And then Elizabeth's child jumps for joy in her womb, and for the first time someone else besides Mary knows who her Child is. Life is different now; nothing will ever be the same again. It's summertime in the history of the world."

"The reading from the Canticle of Canticles at today's Mass is the most beautiful I've ever read," said one of the novices. "*Arise my love, my dove, my beautiful one, and come.*" She paused, hesitant. "*The river is flowing again* – or something like that. How does it go, Mother?"

"*For winter is now past, the rain is over and gone,*" finished Mother Alphonsine.

Just then a wind started up, shaking the branches

of the weeping willow and rippling through the veils and dust cloths of the group. Hands scrambled to keep the needlework in place. Mother Alphonsine looked up at the sky. "You don't think it's going to rain, do you," she said, "on this beautiful day?" She looked up at the clouds overhead. "I think we'd better finish our recreation inside." With haste, she wrapped her embroidery work in her dust cloth and thrust it into her black bag. The novices and postulants did likewise. They folded the wooden chairs and trooped up the path toward the back door of the convent.

THE NEXT DAY at the eleven o'clock instruction, Mother Alphonsine opened the small black book containing the Holy Rule of the Order. "*Particular friendship is the bane of religious life,*" she read. She sat at her desk at the head of the long brown table that filled most of the novitiate room. The fifteen novices and postulants sat on either side of the table, their heads bowed, hands folded on their laps. She closed the book and continued, "Here, we are motivated by sisterly love that reflects the love of God. It is a love that is spread equally among all our sisters." The group remained still, heads bowed. "We never favour one sister over another. This is why we do not speak directly to one another at recreation. We always address the person in charge. This is also why we never go off in twos to discuss anything together. This —" she paused as the word trailed through her teeth like a whistle, "– is why the rule of silence is so precious to us. Silence preserves charity, the charity that we owe to each sister without exception. And that is why we must have the blessing of obedience each time it's necessary to speak to another."

She stopped, and the only sound in the room was the scraping of Annette's chair as she tried to shift closer to Melanie. Mother Alphonsine looked down the table at her. The postulant became still. There was no sound or movement from the group as the novice mistress put down the book and picked up a sheet of paper from her desk. "Our new Holy Father's first encyclical is on truth, unity and peace in a spirit of charity. Most apropos to our instruction this morning." Then she went on: "Listen to what he says about us." She began to read: "'*We must also write of those holy virgins who by their vows have consecrated themselves to God that they might serve Him alone and unite themselves closely with their Divine Spouse in mystic nuptials.*'" She stopped for a moment and looked down the sheet. "'*How much these holy virgins accomplish!*'" she continued. "And he puts an exclamation mark at the end of this sentence." She repeated, her voice in a rise of enthusiasm: "'*How much these holy virgins accomplish!*'"

"Does he say what exactly they accomplish, Mother?" asked Annette suddenly.

There was a barely perceptible turning of heads in the postulant's direction.

Mother Alphonsine pursed her lips and continued reading: "'*They render extensive and distinguished service.*' We all know this: we teach in schools; some sisters work in hospitals, in orphanages, in the missions, in homes for the aged. The Holy Father enumerates all of these and expresses his appreciation for the work that we all do. And he finishes by saying, '*At the same time, they are winning for themselves that imperishable reward which lies ahead in heaven.*'" She looked around the group. "And we do this by pouring ourselves out in love for others so that others may know the love of God. This is why we are here. The sacrifices we make help us to follow this path." She pulled out her watch. "I'll just come quickly to the end before we leave for chapel. He says, '*With all the love of a father, We impart the Apostolic Blessing to each and every one of you, venerable brethren and beloved sons.*' And then it finishes off, '*Written in Rome, on the 29$^{th}$ of June, in the year 1959, the first of Our Pontificate.*' It's signed '*John the Twenty-third.*' And now, praise be to Jesus," she said, making the sign of the cross and picking up her small black book.

The others crossed themselves as well and stood up, putting their chairs under the table. Those along the row by the window stood aside to let Mother Alphonsine pass. At the door, she turned and said, "I'll just have a word with Annette now."

Annette looked around at the others with darting eyes. When she met Melanie's gaze, her face turned into a grimace that emphasized a deep dimple in one cheek. In the corridor, Mother Alphonsine beckoned to her. The novice mistress led the way down the corridor to an alcove where a statue of the patron saint of novices, St. Stanislaus Kostka, stood. The young saint wore the black cassock of a Jesuit and he held a cross to his chest, his eyes raised upward. She drew Annette into the alcove.

The novice mistress pursed her lips again. "I'm sure you meant well in speaking out like that during the instruction, my dear, but you must know that is not how we do things here. Surely you know that by now."

Annette tensed, her hands clasped tightly in front of her. "Yes, Mother."

Mother Alphonsine switched the black book back and forth from one hand to the other. "Are you unhappy here? Do you think you are unsuited to our way of life? Is that why you seem to flout the rules deliberately, even the rules of charity during recreation? Surely you know that when recommendations are made by your superior, they in fact are the will of God. That is why every single thing we do must be done under holy obedience. The will of God exists in the will of the superior. This has been told to you over and over again. So when you disobey the rules in such an open and seemingly deliberate fashion, the only conclusion I can draw is that you are not suited to our way of life." She stopped speaking. "Do you have anything to say?"

Annette moistened her lips with her tongue. "Yes, I know, Mother. It's just that it gets so hard sometimes. Melanie and I were such good friends. You said when we first came here that we'd all be friends. How can we be friends if we can't talk to each other?"

Mother Alphonsine squared her shoulders. "Friendship is a spiritual matter," she said. "Our first friend is Our Lord, and then Our Lady and the saints. Our friendship with our sisters is a spiritual friendship. You must never forget that, my dear."

"I want to do what's right and I want to do God's will, Mother, but I don't understand spiritual friendship," said Annette.

"You will when you've spent enough time in prayer," said Mother Alphonsine. "And then you'll understand that it's only by giving yourself completely, sacrificing your own desires, that you're best able to help others to know and love God. That is the sole reason for the asceticism that we practise here. So you see that friendship as the world understands it is very narrow in its scope and has very little place in our way of life." She smiled. "Time for the visit to chapel. Ask Our Lord to help you."

A MONTH LATER, when the fifteen of them were sitting under the weeping willow in their usual circle, Mother Alphonsine ended the recreation hour by saying, "The postulants will come to the dormitory now to try on their bridal gowns." She folded her needlework inside the dust cloth that had covered her lap and placed it inside her black bag.

"You do remember, don't you," she continued, "that the clothing ceremony is less than two weeks away, and you four will be dressed in bridal gowns to receive your habits from the bishop. You may not know that the gowns have been donated by brides who were graduates of St. Monica's School." A broad smile lit her face. "Of course you're not brides of Christ, not yet at least. That honour is reserved for the novices who are to make their temporary vows of poverty, chastity and obedience at the same ceremony, and it will be your honour in two years." She turned and made her way from the riverbank up to the path. In a flurry of black skirts and folded chairs, the novices and postulants followed.

Inside the novices' dormitory, beds stood in three rows, a chair and bedside stand beside each, the white curtains between the beds held back with ties. At the top of the dormitory, four bridal gowns hung together, white and frothy in a cluster of tulle and lace and satin. The postulants stood in the doorway while Mother Alphonsine and another nun took the gowns, one by one, to the postulants' cubicles. Annette looked around at the other three. When she met Melanie's gaze, she rolled her eyes. Melanie looked down.

"Come and try the dresses on now," said the novice mistress.

The postulants walked to their cubicles and drew the curtains around their beds. The other nun, wearing a blue apron, her veil tied back, walked up and down the row. Around her neck hung a tape measure, and she held a box of straight pins.

One by one, the postulants emerged from behind their curtains. All had taken the black nets off their heads. Carol had struggled to fit a satin gown over her short and stubby frame and now turned around for someone to pull up the back zipper over her undervest.

Mother Alphonsine rushed over to zip her up. Edith stood at the foot of her bed and then bent over, her red-blonde hair falling about her, as she shook out her tulle skirt. Melanie, fixing her long hair with a bobby pin, stood to face the other nun. The bodice of her gown was made of lace and had a scooped neck. The nun knelt in front of her and with long white fingers began fixing a dart at her waist. She gave Melanie a gentle prod to do a half turn.

Annette, in a dress of lace and satin that fit snugly across the bosom, looked at the other three and grinned, showing uneven teeth. The dimple deepened in her cheek. "Aren't we the party princesses," she said.

Mother Alphonsine looked Annette's dress up and down. "Is it too tight, Sister?" she asked the other nun.

"Never!" said Annette. She looked over at Melanie and grinned.

The novice mistress stood erect, reddened, and stared uncharacteristically full-faced at Annette. "We'll have to have these dresses altered and ready before the retreat starts next week," she said.

"Mother, will we have a chance to curl our hair the night before?" asked Carol, by now back in her postulant's dress.

"Of course, my dear." With this response, Mother Alphonsine seemed to regain her composure. "I think that will be all now. The rest of you can get your other clothes back on and I'll see you in the common room in ten minutes."

Back in her cubicle, Annette pulled aside the curtain that separated her cubicle from Edith's. Edith sat on her bed, tucking her hair under her black net. Annette gestured to her to open her curtain on the far side. She hesitated and then drew the curtain. In the far cubicle, Melanie stood with her back to them, her head submerged in yards of white material.

"Mel," said Annette in a loud whisper.

Melanie's head emerged, her hair dishevelled. "I don't know about this," she said. She picked up the gown by the shoulders and held it out at arm's length.

"What do you mean?" Annette whispered.

"Bride of Christ. I don't think I can stand it."

"But we're not brides of Christ. Don't you remember what Mother Alphonsine said? We don't become brides of Christ until we make our vows."

"We're due back in the common room," said Edith as she pulled aside her front curtain.

"We can go along with the dress-up if that's what they want," Annette continued.

Melanie fitted the gown back onto its hanger and hung it on the cubicle rod. "Maybe," she said.

"Do it for God, Mel. That's all that matters anyway," said Annette, her voice briefly muffled as she pulled her postulant's dress over her head. "Can you believe I'm saying this? What would they think over at St. Monica's if they heard me talk like this? Crazy Annette, now the meek and pious nun!" She fixed her net around her hair. "We'd better hurry back."

THE ANNUAL EIGHT-DAY RETREAT began the following week. As recreation drew to a close the evening before, Mother Alphonsine put her needlework down on her lap and looked over the circle around her. "This is our last recreation, all of us together. Do you realize that? Starting from tomorrow we'll be in total silence during the whole of the retreat. It ends the morning of the clothing ceremony. And then those of you who are postulants will be novices, and the novices now preparing for vows will be professed nuns. You will then be with the community, out of the novitiate." The group looked around at each other in silence. "Let us pray for each other as we try to listen to God's voice."

The days of retreat passed. Twice every day they filed into the chapel for the retreat priest's sermon. Each time, he was already kneeling at the altar rail with his back to them. After a few moments he got up and genuflected in a casual way, extending his knee vaguely toward the floor, and then, his black soutane moving in a flourish, he walked over to a small table and chair just inside the sanctuary. He was a tall, broad-shouldered man with a shock of grey hair that fell across his forehead. For each sermon he chose a certain passage from one of the four Gospels. "Now Mary sits at Jesus's feet and listens to Him," said the priest the first day after reading the passage about Martha and Mary from St. Luke's Gospel, "while Martha prepares lunch in the kitchen. Martha gets annoyed at Jesus because He lets Mary sit there rather than telling her to get up and give Martha a hand with the meal. In the Gospel, Jesus says to Martha, 'Mary has chosen the better part.' And then can't we also just imagine Him saying something like, 'For the love of God, Martha, just give me a cup of tea and a sandwich.'" Titters moved through the chapel like a wave.

With each day of silence, unspoken excitement mounted as the ceremony day grew nearer. Pots and boxes of flowers for the altar appeared in the sacristy; china and silverware were laid out in the visitors' auditorium downstairs; from the kitchen came the smell of baking; in the pantry the centre table was laden with tins of cookies and jars of pickles; the visitors' washrooms were scrubbed.

Extra cleaning took the place of the afternoon recreation, and every day Mother Alphonsine assigned a special charge to each of the novices and postulants. One afternoon she told Melanie to mop and dust the small infirmary room down the hall from the novices' dormitory.

The infirmary was actually a bedroom, with a single bed covered with a pink and white checked bedspread, a sink with a towel and washcloth beside it, a chair, a small desk and a closet. The room had a musty smell. Melanie, wearing a wide blue apron over her black dress, with blue cuffs that extended from her wrists to her elbows, ran the feather duster over the windowsill and for a second glanced out the window. Along the street below a young couple walked hand in hand, the young man in a short-sleeved shirt, the girl in a sleeveless blouse and a long flowing skirt. Her hair swung back and forth. Melanie watched them and then closed her eyes quickly and turned away from the window.

She ran the duster over the top of the desk, then moved the mop around the floor, lifting the bedspread to catch the fluff underneath. She glanced at the sink. It had a clean, slightly dusty look, as if it hadn't been used for some weeks.

Beside the sink, the closet door was closed. Melanie cocked her ear for sounds in the corridor. Hearing none, she opened the closet door. Piled up from the floor stood a stack of shoeboxes. Some had been covered with wallpaper scraps. Names were inscribed on the fronts of all of them: the family names of the nuns. One, at the very top of the pile, caught Melanie's eye. It was inscribed Ruth Ann McGinn. She lifted the lid; a white wimple lay there, perfectly arranged, and folded on top, a black veil. Closing the lid, she looked over to the right wall of the closet, where a single habit hung. She reached for it and looked at the initials embroidered on the inside of the neck. The initials were R.A.M.

Sister Ruth Ann, a teacher in the elementary school, had been singled out to the postulants soon after they arrived early in the new year. "Sister Ruth Ann's father is dying over in St. Angela's Hospital," Mother Alphonsine had told them. "Please pray for him."

Every day at recreation they had received an update on the dying man's condition: "Please continue to pray for Mr. McGinn. He is in great pain."

On one occasion she had said, "Please pray that God will take poor Mr. McGinn. This slow agony is so hard on his daughter."

At that point Melanie had piped up: "Does she get over to visit him often?"

"Oh, we don't do that sort of thing," Mother Alphonsine replied. She was working some French knots into a piece of embroidery, twisting her needle round and round the blue thread. She kept her eyes on her needlework and said no more. Silence filled the room.

"Mother, just think of the graces that beautiful sacrifice will earn," one of the novices said.

The nun's father had died not long afterwards. The funeral was held at Purification of Our Lady Church across the street from the convent. The novices and postulants were told that Sister Ruth Ann would not be attending the funeral, but she would be exempted from teaching that day. When they filed out from chapel after Mass, they saw her kneeling in her place near the back. At some point in the morning, they heard the slow toll of the church bell.

Just now, Melanie heard the sound of a small handbell outside in the corridor. She tiptoed out of the closet and closed the door soundlessly. Then she gathered up the mop and feather duster in haste and left the infirmary room. In the corridor, others were making similarly hasty steps toward the novices' linen room to deposit their materials and work outfits in preparation for the afternoon sermon.

ANNETTE SAT BACK ON HER HEELS, wiped the excess dirt from her hand onto her blue apron and then passed the back of her hand across her forehead. It was the last day of the retreat. She and the other postulants had been given the charge of pulling the weeds in the back vegetable garden. She was about to bend down toward the ground again when she heard behind her the sound of someone blowing her nose. She turned around and, squinting in the bright August sunlight, saw Melanie bunching up her large white handkerchief, then putting it back in her pocket. Annette grinned and waved, then squinted more closely. Melanie's eyes were red from crying. Annette shaded her eyes with her hand and looked around the garden for the other two postulants. They knelt up ahead among the peas, Edith's slight frame and Carol's more squat body, pulling and throwing, pulling and throwing, in concentrated rhythm, their backs to Annette and Melanie. Still on her knees, Annette moved backward, lifting her dress over a row of carrots, until she knelt parallel to Melanie. She turned her head toward the other postulant. "Mel, what's wrong?" she whispered.

Melanie sniffed and pulled at a weed.

Annette cast a glance over at the convent and the pathway to the back gate. No one was about. She looked again at Melanie. "Why are you crying?"

Melanie sat back on her heels and blew her nose again. "I'm not sure I can do it," she whispered. Her mouth quivered.

"What are you talking about?" Annette clawed and groped at the ground.

"I don't think I can stand this place any more."

"Don't be silly. What's happened?"

"Do you remember Sister Ruth Ann?" Melanie remained sitting on her heels.

Annette motioned for her to return to her knees. "Sure. She was one of my favourite nuns. What about her?"

"I found her habit in the infirmary closet yesterday."

"So what?"

"Well, you know what that means."

"No, what does it mean?"

"Don't be so thickheaded. It means she's left."

Annette sat up, leaned back and shook her skirt and apron. "What are you talking about?" She now spoke in a normal tone of voice. Melanie put her finger to her lips. Her eyes were dry but still swollen, and she gave a furtive glance about her. "She's gone." Her lips mouthed the words, her voice a bare whisper.

Annette bent down again on all fours and looked at Melanie sideways. "What do you mean? Has she been moved?"

"No! She would still have worn her habit, wouldn't she? She's *left, period.*"

Once again Annette sat up, and then slouched down until her elbows nearly touched the ground in front of her. "No!" She spoke in a loud voice, with an edge of harshness.

Again, Melanie put her finger to her lips. "Yes!" she whispered.

"No!"

"What else can it mean? Why else would her habit be in the closet? All by itself?"

"We have to speak to Mother Alphonsine."

"No! I can't because I didn't have permission to go into the closet. I probably wasn't supposed to see that habit."

"Nuns can't leave just like that. Not after they've made final vows. It would be a mortal sin. They might even get excommunicated from the Church. Sister Ruth Ann would never do that."

There was silence between them. Melanie remained on all fours, motionless, looking down at the ground. Annette moved ahead and began to pull the weeds between the plants.

After a moment, Melanie raised her head. "Annette?"

Annette stood up and stepped over several rows, then knelt down again. She glanced back, shook her head and put her finger to her lips.

AFTER THE NOVICES and postulants had said their late-afternoon rosary in the chapel and were filing into the common room for their evening reading, Mother Alphonsine beckoned to Melanie and drew her into the alcove by the statue of St. Stanislaus.

"Do you have something to report to me?"

Melanie looked at her with a quizzical expression mixed with alarm. "No, Mother?"

Mother Alphonsine's lips were set in a straight line. For a brief moment she said nothing, as if expecting

Melanie to continue speaking. Then, not quite looking at Melanie's face, but at some point midway between her shoulders and the floor, she said, "It's a serious matter to break silence." She paused. "And more serious still to break silence during retreat time." She now let her glance rest squarely on Melanie's face. "But to break retreat silence and not to report this breach of the rule . . ." Melanie looked down and stiffened, then looked up at the novice mistress with tears in her eyes. She bit her lip.

"This is the worst that I've ever seen of postulants breaking the rule of silence. You are never to speak without permission. And to speak to another postulant about a matter that you should discuss with the novice mistress alone! You've been here seven months and you don't know this yet?" Her voice was soft, but there was now a touch of impatience. "You have breached several levels of obedience. Do you realize that? You went into a closet that you should not have gone into – surely you know by now that if you are not explicitly sure that a given action has the blessing of obedience, you must ask. You were told to clean a room. Should you have opened the closet door without permission? No. You always, if in doubt, ask for permission."

Melanie hung her head. Her eyes gazed ahead at the lifeless statue of St. Stanislaus and rested on the shoe protruding like a black triangle from beneath the saint's cassock. "So then you saw something in that closet that made you curious. You should have immediately put the object of curiosity from your mind. You must not dwell on what is not your affair. But failing that – if in spite of your prayer and resolve, you found yourself dwelling on what you saw in the closet, you should have immediately sought me out and told me about it. But you did not. What did you do instead? You told another postulant. Another postulant! Without permission! During retreat silence!" She stopped and looked at Melanie's face once again.

Melanie's gaze remained fixed on the shoe of the statue.

"It will be necessary for you to make reparation for this breach, Melanie. You may still receive the habit, but first you must make reparation before the novices and the other postulants."

Melanie's lips parted only slightly. "Yes, Mother," she said between closed teeth.

"And as for – as for the person you were talking about, pray for her. We do not judge, but we also do not know why she failed in obedience. This is a lesson for us. We never know where one small failing may lead us. We must be constantly vigilant."

An hour later, they moved in their usual line down the back stairs and into the small refectory in the basement. When they had taken their places at the horseshoe-shaped table and Mother Alphonsine had made her way to the head, she said, "Before we say grace, two of the postulants will make reparation. Annette, you may go first."

Annette knelt down in the cramped space, her feet colliding with the wall behind her, and made an effort to face Mother Alphonsine. "In the name of the

Father and of the Son and of the Holy Ghost," she began. "My dear Mother and Sisters, I accuse myself of failing in holy obedience by breaking silence with another person. I ask you to pray for me that I may observe obedience more perfectly in the future." She made the sign of the cross and stood up again. The other novices and postulants stood with their heads down. Edith and Carol looked over at her from the corners of their eyes.

"Melanie?" said Mother Alphonsine.

Melanie knelt down and opened the small piece of paper in her hand. She made the sign of the cross. "My dear Mother and Sisters, I accuse myself of failing in holy obedience. I – I went someplace where I wasn't supposed to go, without permission, and I didn't report it. I broke silence with another Sister and I didn't report it. I ask you to pray for me that I may observe obedience more perfectly in the future. In the name of the Father and of the Son and of the Holy Ghost." She stepped on her skirt and stumbled as she rose to her feet. She blinked her eyes hard and felt in the pocket for her handkerchief as she looked across the table at Annette. Annette's face held no discernible expression.

Mother Alphonsine intoned grace, and stools then scraped the floor as all sat down. She looked over the group. "Any action against holy obedience is of utmost seriousness," she said. "All is forgiven now, of course. It is important to remember, however, that during a retreat before a step is taken in religious life, to break silence is no insignificant matter. However," she continued, looking back and forth over the rims of her glasses at Annette and Melanie, "everything is understood now, and everyone has learned her lesson." She smiled slightly and nodded to the novice at the end of the table as a signal to start serving the meal. Everyone kept their eyes on their plates as they unrolled their cutlery from their napkins. Melanie put her handkerchief in her pocket.

THE NEXT MORNING, the atmosphere bristled with excitement and anticipation and last-minute preparations. Immediately after breakfast, the four postulants, their hair still holding the form of the curlers they had put in the night before, helped with the kitchen wash-up. The air was filled with the smell of a baking ham and the lingering aroma of bread made the day before. From the pantry, nuns carried out stacks of plates, and one stood on a chair to reach a box marked "Priests' Dishes." In the kitchen, Annette had her hands in the sink, washing the fruit bowls, butter plates and bacon pans while Melanie and Carol dried. Edith stood before a large bowl, cutting up cooked potatoes for the visitors' potato salad.

The ceremony was to start at ten o'clock. At half past eight Mother Alphonsine appeared at the kitchen door and moved from one postulant to the other, telling each to finish up quickly and move upstairs. One by one they dried their hands and removed their aprons and blue cuffs.

Upstairs in the novices' dormitory, the four wedding gowns hung beside the postulants' beds. From a hanger just inside the door trailed four long white lace veils. A small swarm of nuns had arrived to help the postulants dress. Mother Alphonsine's usually pale face was flushed and she moved around the dormitory in jerky steps, her arms making flustered arcs.

Melanie hung back as the other three made their way to their cubicles. "Mother," she said as she approached the novice mistress, her voice shaking.

Mother Alphonsine looked down at Melanie's black dress. "Hurry now, Melanie, hurry. There's no time. Hurry and get dressed."

Melanie went to her cubicle and began to undress. From somewhere, a nun held a white petticoat over Melanie's head and dropped it over her shoulders. Then the wedding gown came down around her in a torrent of lacy froth. Behind her, a pair of hands worked the zipper. When she turned around, the nun had disappeared and Melanie stood alone in her cubicle. She put her hand up to her hair, which still held the shape of the curlers, then reached across her bed and opened the curtain an inch. Edith, already dressed, stood with one bare leg on her bed. She was bending over and putting a nylon stocking over her foot when she looked up. Melanie smiled and waved hello, then motioned to her to open the curtain to Annette's cubicle. Edith hopped over and pulled it open a few inches. Annette, struggling to get into her gown with the help of one of the nuns, turned to Melanie, then looked away.

"Annette!" said Melanie in a loud whisper.

Annette turned back and, out of the sight of the

nun, made a motion with her hand for Edith to close the curtain. Edith reached up and drew it back.

Melanie looked at Edith. "What did she do that for?" she whispered.

"We're supposed to be in silence, you know. We don't have permission to talk." Edith's voice was impatient.

"Why can't we talk this morning? We're going to be in silence the rest of our lives, for heaven's sake."

"That's just the point. This is how we are for the rest of our lives. Why should today be any different?" Edith took a comb from her washstand and held it up. "Won't need this much longer," she said, and then left her cubicle for the small mirror at the end of the dormitory.

Melanie sat down in her chair and hoisted up her gown. She still wore her black stockings. She opened her top washstand drawer and rooted past her comb and brush and toothbrush. Then she looked in the drawer underneath. She closed her eyes and then opened them again, looking past the open curtains of her cubicle. The other postulants were jostling each other in front of the small mirror. Annette stood squarely in front, primping her hair. Her satin bodice still strained over her midriff in spite of the alterations that had been made. Sequins sparkled on Edith's gown. Her red-blonde hair had been combed into soft ringlets. Carol stretched and manoeuvred the space to find an opening at the mirror.

Melanie padded toward them in her stocking feet.

"Hurry now, everyone," said Mother Alphonsine.

"Mother, I can't find my nylons," said Melanie.

"Can't find your nylons? Well, I suppose then you can wear your black stockings."

"But won't they show when I'm walking up the aisle? A white gown and white pumps and black stockings?"

Mother Alphonsine took down one of the lace veils and held it up gently. "Annette?" she said.

Annette gave a final pat to her hair and then walked over to Mother Alphonsine, turning her back as the novice mistress placed the veil over her head. Melanie, still standing in her black-stockinged feet, watched. Annette gave Melanie a fleeting glance and as she did so her lips turned up in a slightly crooked smile, the dimple in her cheek deepening for the briefest second. Then her smile disappeared and she looked straight ahead.

"Bride of Christ," said Melanie aloud. "More like the bride of Frankenstein if you ask me."

Heads turned toward her, Mother Alphonsine holding Edith's veil in mid-air.

"Melanie!" Edith gasped.

Melanie reddened. "I'm sorry, Mother. It's just that I was wondering where I could get nylons so that I wouldn't have to wear these into the chapel." She lifted her skirt, showing her black stockings.

Mother Alphonsine, flustered, turned from one side to the other, still holding Edith's veil.

"Here, Mother, I'll do that," said one of the nuns, taking the veil from her and placing it over Edith's head.

Mother Alphonsine disappeared down the corridor. The other three postulants, looking nervous and embarrassed, walked back and forth between the mirror and the door. Melanie hoisted up her skirt and began to march, her feet still encased in black, in imitation of the others, from the door to the mirror and back again.

At the door, she looked up and down the corridor. It was deserted. She headed across to the washroom, stopped and ran down to the infirmary bedroom. In a rush, she opened the door of the room, closed it behind her and then opened the door of the closet. Inside, the boxes with the nuns' family initials were still stacked on the floor. And on top, the box marked R.A.M. She opened the box and ran her fingers over the starched wimple and the thin, smooth veil, and then replaced the lid. She slid her hand down the pile of boxes, squatting, and then kneeling as her hand reached the floor. The tulle skirt of her gown bunched up around her. She reached for the single habit hanging from the overhead rod, and as she did so it came loose from the hanger and fell into a black heap on her lap. She clutched it and buried her face in the coarse material. "No!" she cried, her voice muffled by the folds. She breathed into the habit a moment, and then rose, replaced it on the hanger and shook out her tulle skirt.

She left the infirmary room and walked back toward the dormitory. Mother Alphonsine was standing in the doorway, a pair of nylons trailing from her hand. "Where have you been, child?" she said, handing them to her. "Hurry now, the bishop has arrived. Everyone else is ready. Mother Estelle has started up the organ." Her voice sounded breathless.

The other three postulants stood in single file inside the door, their white lace veils cascading over their shoulders. At the head of the line, Annette smiled, her mouth jerking nervously, her dimple deepening. Melanie returned to her cubicle and sat on her bed.

"Go ahead, Annette." The novice mistress stood aside, her face still flushed.

Annette turned into the corridor and the other two followed.

Mother Alphonsine looked over at Melanie. "Get up, girl!" Her voice was now frantic.

Melanie remained on the bed.

"Come along." Her voice had become a low plea.

Melanie shook her head and stood up. "Please help me undo the zipper, Mother," she said. She turned until her back was toward Mother Alphonsine.

The novice mistress's shaking hands fumbled for the back zipper of the gown. "I don't think you know what you're doing, my dear," she said. Her voice too shook.

Melanie turned and looked at her. The bodice of the gown now fell to her waist. The novice mistress pulled up the fallen shoulders in an effort to cover her. Melanie did not make a move. They looked at each other a long time. The organ could be heard in the distance playing the processional, and still they stood looking at each other. Finally Mother

Alphonsine spoke in a faltering voice, "Has it been too difficult, Melanie? Is that what it is? Should we –" She stopped, her body stiffening.

Melanie opened her mouth to answer, and then turned away from the novice mistress. "I can look after myself now, thank you, Mother. Won't you be needed in the chapel?"

# *Angels of Their Own*

WHEN THE *ding-ding-ding* OF THE NOVICE timekeeper's small handbell sounded in the kitchen doorway, Sister Lucy was standing at the sink, holding the large opaque white bowl in which she had beaten the egg whites for the angel food cake. Rinse water dripped from its rim. A pyramid of kitchen implements had been downturned on the draining tray — the enormous beaters from the electric mixer, various pots and pans, measuring cups and smaller utensils.

At the sharp tinkle of the bell, Sister Lucy's arms jerked to the side in an effort to unburden themselves, and as she set the bowl on top of the pile, the whole mound collapsed in a loud clatter. The bowl slipped from the draining tray and crashed upon the linoleum floor. With shaking hands, her cheeks crimson, she set the draining things aright and, stooping, she scooped up the broken chunks and set them inside her blue apron, holding it like a sack.

In the convent auditorium, Sister Annette saw, rather than heard, the presence of the timekeeper. Keeping a tight grip on the handle of the floor polisher, which tended to glide off on its own like an unruly horse, she had been shifting her gaze back and forth from the floor to the open door at the far end of the auditorium, and in doing so had caught a glimpse of the blue apron and white cotton skirt of the work habit, and the stubby black heel of a shoe. She turned off the machine and took a look around at the stretch of hardwood floor. The shiny circles of polished surface were more evident in some places than in others. She took a deep breath, shrugged and proceeded to unplug the polisher and wind up the cord.

In the chapel, the door opened and the timekeeper's hand reached inside and her finger released the clapper, letting it fall once, *ding,* on the bell's metal rim. Sister Geraldine looked up from the high altar, where she was setting in place the green covering cloth along the altar. The words "Jesus My Lord My God My All" stood out in gold-embroidered letters. She immediately hurried down the steps toward the sacristy door.

Elsewhere, the other seven novices, all dressed similarly in the white broadcloth work habit and white veil, reacted to the bell in much the same way. Outside, those raking the leaves gathered the final bits and pushed them into gunny sacks and hauled them to the side of the shed at the end of the garden. Along the second-floor corridor, others carried mops and brooms, feather dusters and dustpans, to the storage closet across from the linen room. All walked with brisk purpose and intensity of focus, careful not to run, but taking quick steps nevertheless.

"Love; that is why we're here. And that is the essence of the vow of chastity." It was ten minutes later, and Mother Alphonsine, the novice mistress, was speaking from behind the desk where she sat at the top of the novices' common room. The desk was bare except for the white clump of the kitchen bowl's broken pieces in the centre. The novices, now dressed in their black habits, sat in straight-backed chairs on either side of the long brown table. Their hands were folded, fingers interlocking, resting on their laps. They sat upright, looking either downward or straight ahead.

"You know, people in the world can't understand why we are here, why we would shut ourselves up like this," the novice mistress continued. "But what a wonderful sacrifice it is to offer our Saviour. There is so much sin in the world, and so few people who truly love God, who truly love our dear Saviour." The novice mistress's teeth made a clicking sound as she talked, but there was a warm tone in her voice. "Is it too little to ask that I might offer him my entire life, and especially the pinpricks of my life? What does it mean to love? In very practical terms, it means the people around me, my sisters. Which sisters? The sister who is sitting next to me in the refectory. The sister who is rattling her rosary in chapel. Do you remember St. Theresa?" She paused. No one moved. "She was sitting in front of a sister whose rosary was a cause of such distraction as to drive poor St. Theresa mad. And what did she do? She imagined the rattling rosary to be a symphony of music."

Sister Annette unclasped her hands, stretched her fingers, and clasped them again. She moistened her lips with her tongue, breathed out in a silent sigh and lifted her eyes to the window opposite. Outside, the sky was overcast. The top branches of the weeping willow, still a pale green, shook gently in the autumn breeze.

"It's time, Mother," the novice timekeeper said, half rising from her chair at the bottom of the table. In her hand she held the watch that was attached by a black string to the inside of her habit's bodice.

"Quickly, then, Sister Lucy," said Mother Alphonsine.

Halfway down the table, Sister Lucy slid from her chair onto her knees. Her small chin, which almost disappeared within the bounds of the wimple, was on a level with the edge of the table. "My dear Mother and Sisters," she said, making the sign of the cross. "I accuse myself of failing in poverty by breaking a bowl in the kitchen. I ask you to pray for me, that I may observe poverty more perfectly in the future. In the name of the Father and of the Son and of the Holy Ghost."

"Thank you, Sister. Yes, let us try to be more careful with everything we use. You may get up now. And this leads us to tomorrow's instruction – the vow of poverty." The novice mistress tapped the top piece in the pile of broken chunks. "Praise be to Jesus." In a body, all rose and soundlessly placed the chairs back in their places against the table and left in a line for the chapel.

The novices knelt at various places in the front pews and, one by one, stood to make the Way of the Cross. The sound of light rain dripping from the roof echoed through the high space. Weak shafts of light strained through the opaque windows. Under each of the fourteen stations of the cross was written, "We adore thee, Oh Christ, and we praise thee." Silently, walking from station to station, the novices moved their lips or stared impassively at the scenes. Some fingered the rosary beads that hung from their belts. *Jesus falls a first time, a second time, a third time. Veronica wipes His face. Jesus is nailed to the cross, on the ground, spread-eagled. The Roman soldiers, holding hammers, bend over Him on either side. Their legs, criss-crossed with sandal straps, are brown and sturdy. They wear helmets and red cloaks. Jesus is thin, not strong and muscular like the soldiers. He dies. His mother stands beneath the cross, her head bowed under the blue veil. St. John stands beside her. They've been painted with sorrowful faces. Lines have been drawn downward from their eyes and the corners of their mouths. Jesus is laid to rest. A rocky tomb forms the bas-relief of the final station.*

At the fourteenth station, Sister Geraldine stood looking up at the flecks of dark brown paint dabbed onto the lighter brown of the rock when a voice beside her began singing in a loud whisper: "Juzz ma *Lawd,* ma *Gawd,* ma *A-w-w-wl.*" The tune was that of the Protestant hymn "Just a Closer Walk with Thee," and it was Sister Annette standing beside her, exaggerating a low southern drawl, the deep dimple in her cheek twitching. She looked at Sister Geraldine, lifting her eyebrows up and down like a slapstick comedian, and jerked her head toward the altar. Sister Geraldine turned and followed the direction of her nod. The green altar covering was crooked at the far end and the fold at the gold-embossed word "Jesus" covered up two of the letters, so that, from the far right side of the chapel, where the two novices stood, the name of Jesus looked to be "Jus." As the handbell sounded – again, another single *ding* – Sister Geraldine opened the communion rail gate, lifted the front of her skirt, sprinted up the steps to the altar and gave a swift swipe across the cloth to smooth it out.

"TODAY WE WILL TALK about the vow of poverty," Mother Alphonsine said the next day. She held a small black New Testament in a hand that was half covered with the sleeve of her habit. Her index finger held the book slightly open. The pieces of the broken bowl had disappeared from her desk. "Poverty is the virtue and the vow by which I acknowledge to Almighty God that I am nothing and I have nothing. And how do I do this? I come to God with empty hands. I have no possessions. Anything I use, whether it is a pen or a book or an article of clothing, belongs to the community. It is for my use only. I own nothing. Everything is held in common. We live like the early Christians who are described this way in the Acts of the Apostles." She opened her New Testament to the place her finger held and looked down her glasses. "*And all they that believed, were together, and had all things common. Their possessions and goods they sold, and divided them to all, according as every one had need. And continuing daily with one accord in the temple, and breaking bread from house to house, they took their meat with gladness —*" she closed the book slowly and looked up — "*and simplicity of heart.*" She moved her head back and forth, surveying the novices in front of her. "And the result? What is the result, Sister Geraldine? What is the result of our vow of poverty?"

Sister Geraldine turned toward the novice mistress, her hands still clasped in her lap. Her pale face and washed-out blue eyes with their sparse, light lashes gave the impression of a blank white page. "Mother, we should be filled with joy in offering Our Lord everything. We have nothing, Mother. We try to be poor, to show ourselves as nothing."

"Mother." It was Sister Annette, speaking from across the table. Eyes moved in her direction, and heads turned almost imperceptibly at this intrusion into the novice mistress's daily instruction. Mother Alphonsine's eyes widened and she held her head erect as she looked down the table at the novice.

"Mother, there's just something I've been wanting to ask." Sister Annette leaned over, looking directly at Mother Alphonsine. "Why do we have to darn our stockings till there's hardly any stocking left, there's just one big wad of darning cotton covering our feet? I mean, what does that have to do with poverty? It would be a lot less expensive just to buy new stockings."

Mother Alphonsine's eyes remained widened and she answered in a bland voice, trying to hold down a tone of exasperation. "Here, Sister, we come to '*holy* poverty.' By holy poverty we try to take care of the goods that we use. I do not simply throw something away because it is worn out or broken. I try to mend it, fix it. This is what it is to be truly poor."

Sister Annette remained bolt upright, her head turned toward the novice mistress. She wet her lips as if trying to decide whether to interrupt the instruction further. "But Mother —" she began.

"All right, Sister, I'd say that's enough for today." Mother Alphonsine straightened the New Testament, aligning it against an invisible mark. She ran a finger down its edge and then up again. "We will now move on to obedience."

Sister Annette once again faced front, her eyes cast downward.

"It is important to remember that in obedience we do not contradict the superior. In obedience it is necessary to suspend my own inclinations and my own desires and feelings for the good of the community, to submit my will to that of the superior. This is the most difficult thing in the world to do, and don't let anyone tell you that it isn't. If you can live a life in perfect obedience to your superior, this is a holy life. A saintly life."

She dropped her hands to her lap. "Now," she said, her voice sounding more sprightly. "Today is the first of October, and this means –" she paused. Heads again turned in her direction. "Starting on the first of October we go outside with our overshoes on and our shawls around our shoulders. We continue this practice, regardless of the weather, until obedience tells us we may go outside *without* our overshoes and shawls. This of course will be sometime in the spring. It's for health reasons that we do this practice of course – the vineyard of Our Lord needs strong, healthy women, not sickly souls. But more deeply and more importantly, we do it because obedience has said so, and our actions must always be blessed by obedience." She shot a quick glance in the direction of Sister Annette, who made no gesture or perceptible response. From across the table, the novice timekeeper had slipped her watch out from inside the bodice of her habit. "Of course there is also the Holy Angels Tea tomorrow, and we will speak about this at recreation. Praise be to Jesus."

"It's the feast of the Holy Guardian Angels tomorrow, Mother!" said Sister Geraldine when they were settled at afternoon recreation in their usual semicircle around the novice mistress. Sister Geraldine was smiling now, her face more animated than it had been at the instruction, and less pale.

The brown table now stood across the back of the common room, and a wide strip of white paper lay on it. The words "WELCOME *to the* HOLY" already appeared in thick black letters on the paper, as well as the letter *A,* and Sister Lucy stood before it with a paintbrush filling in the letter *N*. Working beside her, Sister Annette drew gold shadowing along the letters with a thin brush. Each of the others, including Mother Alphonsine, held a stylized paper angel with stiff, stand-out wings. They were preparing to add faces to them.

"That's right, and that means – the Holy Angels Tea," said Mother Alphonsine. The novice mistress was working with a pen on her angel. "And some of you will be helping out with the tea preparations tomorrow. Just in the kitchen, of course. Canon Law doesn't allow novices to intermingle with seculars. There," she said, turning her paper angel around. It had slits for eyes and an upturned line for a mouth.

"She looks like the cat that got the canary, Mother," said one of the novices.

The novice mistress held the paper angel at arm's length, scrutinizing it. "These will make pretty centrepieces," she said.

"As long as you make them all happy rather than grumpy," said Sister Annette, looking up from the back table. "Let's not have a tongue sticking out, Mother."

"Mother, why do they have a tea on the feast of the Holy Angels?" one of the novices asked.

"It's for the alumnae of St. Monica's. They love to come back and see their old teachers again."

"But Mother, why the Holy Angels?"

"I'm not sure. The origin of the tea is lost in the mists of time. Perhaps because St. Monica put her son, St. Augustine, into the care of his guardian angel, and look what happened to him – he came from being one of the worst sinners in the Church to being one of the greatest saints."

"It's so comforting to think of a guardian angel, isn't it, Mother?" another novice said.

Mother Alphonsine had started in on another paper angel. "Yes, especially when you think of angels appearing in Sacred Scripture just when needed – there's Jacob's angel, Tobias's angel, angels ministering to Jesus in the desert –"

"What Jesus said about angels in the gospel for tomorrow's feast," said Sister Lucy from the back of the room. "'*Woe to those who scandalize children. These little ones have angels of their own in heaven –* '"

"Holy *Angles?!* Holy *Angles?!*" Sister Annette, looking down at the black letters with widened eyes, stood back from the table, her gold-tipped brush poised in her hand.

Sister Lucy looked at the letters and read aloud slowly, "A-N-G-L –" She put her hand up to her mouth and then raised her eyes and let out a loud groan. The novices turned around to look, the paper angels aflutter in their hands.

Mother Alphonsine swallowed and took a few seconds before speaking, and then said in a controlled voice, "We can glue another paper on top. It's just the two letters that need to be switched around –"

"Sister Lucy should think of Jell-o, Mother," said one of the novices. "Only *g* instead of *j* of course."

"Yes, well, we don't have much time."

Sister Lucy stared at the novice mistress, a look of grief on her face.

"Don't cry over spilled milk, Sister," Mother Alphonsine said. "Put another paper on top and do the letters over again."

Sister Annette stood stiffly at attention, impersonating a butler. "Welcome, Ladies, to the Holy Angles Tea!"

THE NEXT AFTERNOON five novices worked at the kitchen sideboard. Sister Annette stood before the whirring electric mixer. Sister Geraldine and two others were cutting the crusts off the sandwiches, slicing the pinwheel rolls and arranging them on doily-covered plates. Sister Lucy was sawing carefully back and forth into the angel food cake.

"Hi, Sister!" The voice came from the kitchen door, shattering the silence, and the novices turned around, startled. A stout woman with graying hair stood there, wearing a blue felt hat, tan coat and large plastic earrings that clung to her earlobes. She wore tight-fitting patent-leather shoes and carried a matching handbag. Her ruddy face beamed with a jolly smile.

"So this is where you Sisters do your magic work," she said. She took a step inside the kitchen.

"Look at those pretty sandwiches! Oh, and look at this! Your famous angel food cake! A mile high and light as a feather, I'll bet."

Sister Annette bowed low over the mixer, and the others looked at one another and tittered nervously. Sister Geraldine grabbed the skirt of her apron and then let go in jerky alternate movements. "I'll get Mother," she said in a breathless whisper to the novice beside her, and slid out the door.

"And I know what's over there! It's the cream getting whipped for the angel food, isn't it?" Still beaming, the woman click-clacked in her high heels toward Sister Annette. The smell of perfume floated behind her. The other novices followed her with their eyes and smiled like schoolchildren watching a misdemeanour in the act.

"There goes my diet!" Her voice boomed above the noise of the electric beaters, and as she came alongside Sister Annette, she slipped her index finger inside the bowl. It re-emerged with a wad of whipped cream, which she lifted to her mouth. Stifled giggles shot through the cluster of novices behind her.

Sister Annette turned toward the woman. "Hi, Mrs. Maloney," she said in a quiet voice.

The woman's mouth fell open, the whiteness of the whipped cream tracing lines along the pale pink of her tongue. "An-*nette!*" She flung her arms open and reached toward the novice. Sister Annette stood with her arms at her sides as the tan coat and patent-leather purse enveloped her, and she looked over the woman's shoulder at the other novices, her eyes wide, the dimple in her cheek deepening, her face a question mark.

The woman stood back to survey her. "Well, I'll be! *Look* at you! Dressed just like the nuns!"

Sister Annette opened her mouth, uncertain of how to proceed, her uneven teeth catching her bottom lip. "Yes, well I got the habit a month ago. Everything's the same as the nuns' habit, except our veil is white." She gave her veil a gentle tug to make her point.

"Well, of course, I remember when you entered last January. You and another girl from St. Monica's."

"Yeah. Melanie. She left."

"She left? Why?"

"Well, I guess she figured she wasn't meant for this life. This is really a testing time." The novice's voice had become barely audible over the electric mixer.

Sister Lucy looked over at the two of them, her eyes wide. "What are we supposed to do?" the novice beside her whispered. Sister Lucy gave a quick shrug of her shoulders and put extra concentration into the slicing of the angel food cake. Suddenly, a bright balloon of blood rose from her thumb. She gasped out loud and jumped back. With her other hand she pulled out a large white handkerchief from her pocket and pressed it to the bleeding cut.

"Let's have a look." The woman had released Sister Annette and was at Sister Lucy's side. "Oh, why do they make you girls use these great big men's hankies? They're so unsanitary. I bet you've got five days' worth of snot on that thing." She grabbed the handkerchief and threw it to the floor, by now holding Sister Lucy's hand firmly in her own. "Let me see if I have a Band-Aid." She dropped the hand, and Sister Lucy put her thumb to her mouth and pressed her tongue against it. The woman rummaged in her purse for a Band-Aid. Visible inside the bag were a worn brown wallet, a package of cigarettes, a tube of lipstick and a school picture of a teenaged girl. She dug deeper and pulled out a single Band-Aid. "O-kay," she said as she pulled down the tiny red thread to loosen it. "Let's see that thumb." Sister Lucy rubbed her thumb against her apron and then held it up toward the woman. "There we are," the woman said as she affixed the tape around the thumb. "Good as new."

Sister Lucy murmured, "Thanks," and looking furtively at the woman, bent down to pick up her handkerchief. The woman, noticing the picture of the girl inside her purse, pulled it out and turned back to Sister Annette, who had finished whipping the cream and was at the sink, rinsing the beaters. In the picture, the girl wore the St. Monica's school uniform and her dark blonde hair was held in place by a small barrette.

"Oh, Annette. Here's the last picture we have of Cathy. This was just before — she was taken to hospital."

Sister Annette turned off the tap. She held up her hands to show the woman their wet condition, and thus her inability to take the picture. "Actually, Mrs. Maloney —" she hesitated. "— you're not really supposed to be in here. This is part of the cloister."

The picture dangled from the woman's hand. She looked around, one side of her lipsticked mouth drooping open. The kitchen was filled with tomblike silence. Even the cutting and slicing sounds had been suspended. The novices stood in stiffened embarrassment, facing the sideboard. "People aren't allowed in here," Sister Annette continued. Her voice was gentle and her face had a look of unaccustomed seriousness. "Except the nuns."

The woman slowly returned the picture to her purse. "Cathy used to talk sometimes about wanting to become a nun," she said. She turned and walked with slumped shoulders toward the door, her purse hangdog in her hand. The back of her coat sagged.

Sister Annette hesitated and then wiped her hands on her apron and hurried after the woman. "Mrs. Maloney." She stopped and then started again. "Mrs. Maloney. May I see that picture of Cathy, please?"

In the doorway the woman turned back, and as she did so, Mother Alphonsine appeared with Sister Geraldine behind her. The novice mistress smiled at the woman and swung her arm in a wide arc around her, steering her away. "We'll be bringing the tea out in just a few minutes, Mrs. Maloney," she said in a soothing voice.

Beyond the kitchen wall, the chattering of women's voices had begun. "Oh, we have quite a nice crowd of ladies . . ." Mother Alphonsine was saying.

The timekeeper appeared with her bell and gave a brisk *ring-a-ling* at the kitchen door. Mother Alphonsine reappeared and said, "Leave everything now. It's time for the instruction. The nuns from St. Monica's will be serving the tea, and they'll finish up the preparation in here." She turned to Sister Geraldine. "That was the right thing to do, Sister, coming to get me." Sister Geraldine bowed her head and said, "Thank you, Mother."

Sister Annette gave a sharp bang to the beaters on the edge of the sink to relieve them of the last vestiges of whipped cream. She banged them a second time, and then a third, in spite of their already being clean, before setting them on the draining tray.

Sister Lucy stood looking at a slice of angel food cake that lay on the cutting board. Its perfect whiteness was marred by a ragged bloodstain. Then, in a gesture of unusual energy, she lifted the cutting board and scraped the piece of cake into the scrap pail. Looking around to check if anyone was watching her, she saw that Sister Annette still faced the sink. Everyone else had left the kitchen, and the plates of fancy sandwiches stood half filled. Sister Lucy thrust her hand into the pail and shoved the angel food slice out of sight below the slops and peels.

# *O Come Emmanuel*

SISTER LUCY HURRIED DOWN THE CORRIDOR toward the novices' common room, aware that she wasn't as recollected as she should have been, but at this moment she didn't care. Her eyelids fluttered, and her shallow breathing and the tiny tap-tap sound of her rubber-soled shoes on the hardwood floor reflected the anxiety that was just now hitting at the centre of her chest.

Inside the common room, she picked up a sheet of paper from a stack on the long brown table, sat at her desk and began to write.

*"Dear Mum and Dad and Charlie. I'm writing this letter a day ahead of time: Instead of writing our letters home on the first Sunday of the month as we usually do, we're writing them today because tomorrow Advent begins, and we —"* She paused and then began to write again: *"we're —"* She was about to write *"we're not allowed"* when just in time she realized she mustn't use the

word "allowed" because it suggested that external constraints were being placed upon the novices, when in fact they were learning that inner discipline was the key to following the rules of religious life. She wrote instead, *"we're not writing home during Advent."*

She stopped and sat back, feeling for a brief second a sense of self-mastery. She had been in the convent almost two years now, and it was good to feel from time to time that she belonged. It was no longer a matter of being allowed to do this, or not being allowed to do that. She was one of the nuns now – well, not exactly one of them, she was still only a novice and thus wore a white veil rather than a black one, but she wore the habit now, and anyone from the outside looking at her would call her a nun. Even her mother's letters now addressed her as, *"My dear daughter, Sister Lucy."* She no longer belonged to her family, even though, of course, she loved them. But she had joined the band of women who were intent on a life of Christian perfection. Mother Alphonsine, the novice mistress, said that the Holy Father himself had praised all the nuns in the world, referring to them as "the flowers of the Church."

Sister Lucy opened up the top of her desk and pulled out last month's letter from her mother. On the envelope she had written a list of four items: St. Stanislaus feast; joke about Rudolph; tablecloth; Advent & Xmas. She had begun compiling a list every month of things to tell her family, because when letter-writing Sunday came around it was difficult to know on the spur of the moment what to write about. So little happened in the novitiate that was out of the ordinary. The list helped her remember the few events in her life that might prove interesting to her family.

The novices had been told not to write of matters that concerned internal dealings of the convent. Mother Alphonsine, the novice mistress, said that people who still lived in the world didn't understand the spirit of religious life. Once, Sister Lucy had written to her parents that she was wearing holes at the knees in her stockings from kneeling so much. *"We even kneel when we're eating sometimes!"* she had written, intending it as a joke (although this was a practice that actually took place once or twice a week as a penance). Mother Alphonsine, who read all the novices' letters, incoming and outgoing, had asked her to write the letter over again and to write nothing about knees and holes in stockings. She had complied without protest, her face burning with humiliation. Although Mother Alphonsine had spoken kindly to her, Sister Lucy felt she had somehow shamed herself in her gauche way of trying to write something lighthearted. She had replaced the offending passage with, *"We're sure doing a lot of praying."* Then she had added, lest Mother Alphonsine think she was complaining, *"We pray for our families especially, and also for priests in the foreign missions."*

She now began to write again. *"We had a really nice surprise on November 13. It was the feast of St. Stanislaus. St. Stanislaus is the patron saint of novices. He was a novice in the Jesuit Order, and he died while he was still a novice.*

*We had jam for breakfast and we didn't have to do chores in the morning or the afternoon. We spent the morning having a singalong and the afternoon playing Scrabble. The nuns fixed up the novitiate common room for us to look like a garden, with flowers all over the place. Was it ever pretty!"*

Sister Lucy looked ahead at the white veil of the novice in front of her. The novice's head was bent, the middle crease in the veil folded just so, then opening and falling over and down her back. Sister Lucy followed the crease with her eyes. What more could she write about the feast of St. Stanislaus that would be of interest to her parents and younger brother? They had no idea what it had meant to come upon an unexpected oasis in the midst of a barren landscape. Not that life in the convent was barren: on the contrary, the simplicity and starkness of religious life spoke of the one thing necessary, which was to love God and Him alone, to pare yourself down to nothing but essentials, to gird yourself and follow Jesus. That was the whole point of giving up your life in the world, and saying goodbye to your family and your dog and your bedroom with the frilly pillows and your collection of stuffed animals. That was the point of six hours in chapel each day, of learning the Holy Rule of the Order.

But November seemed to drag on forever, each day like the day before it, grey and drafty, with no feast day to bring new flowers to the chapel and a special dessert for dinner. And then on the night of November 12, a day which means nothing to anyone, a handful of nuns had left night prayers, and in the convent's Great Silence had transformed the bare novitiate common room into a parkland. They had strung garlands around the room, hung baskets heavy with flowers, created a rock garden and cobblestone paths by artfully crumpling brown paper. And at the top of the room, replacing the novice mistress's desk, a huge box had been transformed into a horse and carriage. On each novice's desk sat a small potpourri that contained a tiny rolled-up piece of paper. Inside was a message, individually typed, from St. Stanislaus that Sister Lucy supposed Mother Alphonsine had composed. Her message had read, *"Dear Sister, May God fill you Himself, not according to your fears and weaknesses, but according to the measure of His Love. May He increase your confidence, that it may enlarge in you the capability of more fully possessing Him and of loving Him more deeply."*

If she wrote about such things in her letter, she could imagine her father shaking his head and muttering, "What are they doing to her in that place?" Her mother would smile a sweet, sad smile, and her brother Charlie would stamp out of the room with his finger shoved down his throat. They could not begin to understand. And what if she told them that they had played Scrabble and volleyball in silence? Her father and brother would only laugh at her if she said it felt like a strange experience, but in fact was actually not so bad – rather like getting used to sitting up straight all the time and not crossing your legs.

She looked at her list and began to write again. *"Here's a joke one of the novices told us. It's a little early for*

*Christmas, but here goes. Question: What is Santa's other reindeer called? Answer: Olive. Do you get it? (Clue: Olive = 'All of').*" She continued: "*Do you remember the tablecloth I told you I was embroidering at recreation? Well, I'm almost finished it, and it has light blue flowers and pretty red baby cardinals.*"

She looked up again from her letter. Around the room, the other novices were bowed over their desks. At the front of the room stood the novice mistress's desk. On the desk was a Bible and the black-bound copy of the Order's Holy Rule. Behind the desk and the empty chair of the novice mistress hung the large picture of the Sacred Heart, Jesus pointing to his heart with his eyes raised to heaven. To the right, facing out to the room, stood a statue of St. Roch. He wore tattered clothes and both legs were bare, and on one thigh was a red gash. Beside him, on the same plaster base, stood a statue of a dog. Mother Alphonsine had told the novices the story of St. Roch: during the great plague of Europe he had helped look after the sick with tireless devotion until one day he himself took sick and was turned out of town. Alone and friendless, he had crawled into a forest, where a dog licked his wounds, nursing him back to health. At first, the sight of St. Roch's statue had shocked Sister Lucy, but day after day of facing it and the picture of the Sacred Heart and reciting the "Come, Holy Ghost" before the morning instruction had given her a familiarity with it. In fact, she enjoyed looking at the thick red painted line at the top of St. Roch's leg. Some days it seemed longer and more slender than others. Some days it seemed to point up at the Sacred Heart, and on others it seemed to have sprouted little pimples that pierced the dark beige flesh of the leg.

Mother Alphonsine had gone on to tell them how he had healed a former Reverend Mother of tuberculosis. She had been near death as a novice, spitting blood and gasping for air. Someone had placed a relic of St. Roch on her chest. The next morning her lungs were clear and she lived a long and saintly life, dying when she was ninety.

Some of the novices had been skeptical about the story. "What was the relic, Mother?" Sister Pauline had asked, "A piece of bone? It would be pretty dried up, I guess. And how would they know it came from St. Roch if the only friend he had was a dog?"

"Maybe the relic was a piece of cloth dipped in the blood that dripped from his wound that got licked by the dog . . ." said another novice.

"That came from the house that Jack built," finished Sister Pauline in a mock singsong voice. Titters rippled through the group. Mother Alphonsine said nothing.

Sister Lucy had thought the story of the miraculous cure was inspiring and she felt confused by the other novices' banter. She had imagined herself as the pale, tubercular novice lying on a simple cot, deeply serene in spite of wracking pain. Sister Pauline tended to be a little disrespectful, perhaps even irreverent at times, she thought, but in spite of herself, Sister Lucy liked her. Sister Pauline had a twinkle in her eye and an easy smile. Sister Lucy had decided to disregard the remark about St. Roch's relic, as Mother Alphonsine had done.

She looked back at her letter now, turning her pen over in her hands. She was wasting time. Soon the bell would ring and the novices would have to hand in their letters and then scatter to do the rest of the day's chores. It was easier to think, to reflect, than it was to write.

Then she remembered one more thing about the feast of St. Stanislaus and once more began to write. "*We had a record of songs by Mario Lanza while we played games in the afternoon.*" The songs had been an unusual intrusion of worldliness in the silence of the novitiate. Sister Lucy now remembered how Mother Alphonsine had moved smoothly over to the record player as Mario Lanza was belting full throttle, "Be my lo-o–ove, for no one else can fil-l-l this year-r-rning . . ." and had lifted the needle and turned the record over, saying in a bland voice, "Perhaps we'll hear the other side now." Something had lurched inside her chest at that moment, and for no reason she could explain to herself, her eyes had burned with sudden tears. Then the moment had passed and she had returned her attention to the Scrabble board as in the background familiar organ music swelled and Mario Lanza's voice burst into the "Ave Maria."

She now breathed a deep sigh and sat back in her seat, filled with self-disgust. She had almost exhausted her list of items and had filled little more than half a page. Turning over the envelope, she looked at her mother's handwriting. *Sister Mary Lucy.* Her mother's pride in every word. She opened the letter.

*Well, it seems like a long time since we heard from you. Last month, wasn't it? Ha, ha. You'd think by now I'd learn that you are writing to us every month.*

*Everything is fine here. Your father took up the last of the leaves last week, and we had a huge bonfire. You would have loved it, the flames and the sparks and everything. Mrs. Shapcott says that she misses you at the Girls' Club. She misses the way you helped to clean up her kitchen after making the muffins and things. She says the other girls don't do very much work at all. She's such a fuss-budget that I thought it was nice that she had something nice to say about you. It kind of surprised me.*

*I made the Christmas cake last week too, so now it's soaking in brandy!! And same as last year, I missed your help in measuring the fruit and the spices. I don't know when I'll stop missing you. Maybe never! But I shouldn't talk like this, it will only make you lonesome. But you're happy there with the nuns, and that makes me happy.*

*Charlie lost out on last month's spelling bee because he spelled hemorrage wrong. Or maybe it was hemorroid. I forget, but it was one of those words that have an extra h somewhere. As you can see, I don't have the spelling right either!! Well, I can tell you I nearly had a hemhorrage or a hemhorroid myself when I saw him straining to try and get it. Poor Charlie! He misses you, though as you know he'd never admit it. I don't think I have those words spelled right yet. I just don't know where that extra h goes. Oh Well. My daughter the* NUN *may be able to set me straight.*

*Between you and me, Sister Lucy, I don't want to worry you, but your father goes to the Legion a lot at night and I don't like it too much. You know, he likes to be with his buddies that he was in the war with, and what can I do about that? I think he misses you too. It makes me kind of lonesome in the evenings, tho with the new TV I can watch the programs and do my knitting. I'm knitting Charlie a sweater for Christmas. He's growing so fast that I'm afraid it may not fit him. Or maybe I'll make it too big and the arms will hang down past his hands! But look at me, going on and on about nothing. It's just kind of nice to write to you. It almost feels like I'm talking to you right here in the kitchen. Oh yes, pray for Father Mulvihill. He's had a stroke and can't do much any more, poor man. You know how he used to like visiting people's homes. But now he can't get around any more. He has to sit in that cold rectory. The ladies take turns doing the housecleaning for him . . .*

Father Mulvihill. Sister Lucy remembered the time, just before her First Communion when she was six years old, when the priest had dropped in to visit, as he often did. It was early summer and two nuns had come out from the city to teach catechism to the country children. It was the first time she had seen nuns close up, and she spent the catechism days looking at the starched linen that wound around their faces. The nuns had a clean, soapy smell. The dead heat and the buzzing flies didn't seem to bother them; they always looked fresh in their bulky clothes.

She had learned all the necessary prayers from the nuns, and her mother, putting the kettle on the stove, said to her in front of the priest, "Say the Act of

Contrition for Father." The ironing board was still up, her mother having just done the final sewing and pressing on her First Communion dress. The dress hung from the top of the pantry door, shimmering and lovely. She herself had picked up a large scrap of the white material from the floor and was holding it in her hand.

"What are you going to do with that?" Father Mulvihill asked. His trouser legs were dusty from the dirt road leading to their house, and his shoes were scuffed.

"I'm going to make a First Communion dress for Diane," she answered.

"Father," her mother prompted.

"Father."

"Who's Diane?" he asked. Sister Lucy couldn't remember if the priest really cared or was merely absent-minded.

"My doll," she said. "Father," she added, looking at her mother. Diane was the prettiest name she had ever heard in her six years of life.

"Say the Act of Contrition for Father," her mother said again.

"*Oh my God, I am heartily sorry for having offended Thee. And I detest all my sins –*" She continued through the rote prayer, and her mother smiled at Father Mulvihill with relief when she had completed it – "*I firmly resolve with the help of Thy grace to confess my sins, to do penance, and to amend my life amen.*" – without pause or error.

He said, "Good girl." He spoke with no real interest, but with a gentle kindliness. For her mother, it was important only that he should be sitting in their kitchen hearing her prayers. For her mother, the priest's presence transformed the kitchen.

The nuns did not come to visit. They boarded with an old widow in the village and went back and forth from the widow's house to the church every day. "Your souls will be whiter than your dresses," said one of the nuns, referring to the state of grace they'd be in after making their First Confession, after they'd made their Act of Contrition for real. Sister Lucy had always remembered that – in fact, it was the only thing she remembered from that week of catechism before her First Communion – and now here she was, wearing the habit of the very same nuns.

Her mother's signature. *Love, Your Mother.* She looked around at the other novices, their heads bent, their pens scratching on paper, and then at the picture of the Sacred Heart on the wall at the top of the room. Jesus's finger pointed to the thorns circling His heart and the three drops of blood that fell from it. One drop for her mother, sitting alone. One for poor Father Mulvihill. One for her father – what was her mother implying in her letter that she did not say? Three drops of blood. None left for Charlie, who would be opening Christmas presents by himself again this year. Her eyes were riveted to the heart of Jesus in the picture. She closed them to get the image out of her mind. It unnerved her; it was too real looking, that heart. It should have been like the heart of Jesus on statues, red, like a valentine. Not like a real heart. With her eyes closed, she could hear pulsating sounds inside her head. Something was throbbing throughout her body, inside her head and her chest.

Just then an ancient, melancholy melody came to her mind and she began whistling it quietly through her teeth. It was a piece of Advent music the novices had begun practising yesterday afternoon. Mother Estelle, the brisk music mistress, had swept into the gloomy half-light of the basement music room with an armload of sheet music and had arranged herself on the piano stool. The novices were already seated, their chairs in a large semicircle around the piano.

"Advent," the nun had announced. "We're preparing for the coming of the Lord." She began to trace a melody on the piano with her right hand, then swivelled around to face the novices. She fixed her eyes at a point on the wall behind them.

"This is glorious music," she said, "magnificent in its simplicity. *Veni, veni, Em-man-u-el.*" She said the words slowly, exaggerating the syllables. "*O come, O come, Emmanuel.* It's the cry of longing for the Savior. In the flow of the music you can feel the centuries of exile and sadness."

Sister Lucy looked out the window at the bare bushes that seemed stuck into the earth like sticks against the overcast late November sky. Nothing was visible beyond them. She longed for either sunshine or darkness. Sunshine always made things seem bright; darkness brought bedtime and the oblivion of sleep. The grey half-light made her feel empty and desolate.

"*Veni, veni O O-riens. O come, Thou Day-spring from on high. Dis-perse the glo-o-omy clouds of night.*" Mother

Estelle recited the words as if they were poetry, her eyes roaming back and forth along the wall behind the novices. Sister Lucy stared at her with resentment. She had hoped they'd practise Christmas music, something pretty that would make her feel better. She hated the intense look in the nun's eyes, the deliberate slowness of her speech.

"We'll be singing it in Latin, of course," Mother Estelle went on, "but you almost don't need a translation because you can feel the yearning here, in the rise and fall of the chant itself. Do you hear it? *Death's dark shadow put to flight.*"

She turned away from them, facing the piano keys, and again played the melody with her right hand. She turned her head around as far as it would go and looked at the floor over her shoulder as she sang, "*Diras-que noc-tis te-nebras.*" She stopped suddenly and turned around again, this time looking directly at the semicircle of faces.

"Does anyone know what 'Emmanuel' means?" she asked, her eyes moving from one novice to the next. Sister Lucy ran her tongue over her bottom lip. It felt dry and cracked.

"'Emmanuel,'" the nun said to the silent group, "means 'God with us,' and this is what we're praying for, for ourselves and for all people during Advent: we're praying for God to be with us. We're in lonely exile, every one of us, and we long desperately for the link that will unite us with the divine. The simplicity of this music helps us to express that longing like nothing else can. Now let me hear you sing." She rearranged herself on the piano stool and once again her hand came down upon the keys.

The novices picked up their music from their laps and began to sing. In the unison of the voices around her, surrounded by the unfamiliar Latin words, Sister Lucy felt for a moment that she was not alone, that in the longing that seemed to fill her emptiness she belonged to every other person who ever lived. The moment passed, but recalling it now, as the music rose and fell inside her, beyond rhythm or tune, she felt them all there – her mother, her father, Father Mulvihill. Charlie. Herself with them as well.

The bell rang, startling her. Her quiet whistle fell silent. Around her, the other novices rose and placed their letters in unsealed envelopes on the novice mistress's desk. She watched Sister Pauline get up, the rosary at her side swaying jauntily against the perfect folds of her habit skirt.

Sister Lucy bent over her letter one last time. "*I've got to go now. I pray for you all, Mum, Dad and Charlie, and for Father Mulvihill. I pray that God will be with us all. I won't be with you for Christmas, but inside our hearts we'll all be together. Bye-bye.*" She hesitated a moment. She had written nothing of what she really felt, but how could she say it? There weren't enough words in the whole world, and besides, the bell had sounded. Holding her pen tightly, she wrote, "*From your loving daughter, Sister Lucy.*"

As she folded her letter, she looked up and saw that Sister Pauline was trying to catch her eye. Then the other novice winked, brought up her hands in a back-and-forth cheerleading gesture, palms facing front, and did a quick skip backward, like a dance step. Sister Lucy's face stretched into a smile. Her cheek muscles felt strained for a second, then they relaxed. She realized it was the first time she'd smiled all day.

## *Holy Innocents*

THE VOICES BEGAN SOFT AND SUBDUED, AS was normal behind closed doors, but one voice began to rise and became sharp and staccato, and then erupted: "She said *no!* Just like that!" The other voice said, "S-h-h-h – we –" Then they were indistinct again. The figures in shadow behind the frosted window of Mother Estelle's music room gave no hint of whom the voices belonged to.

Sister Geraldine had stiffened at the sound, and the mop handle she was holding jerked back and forth on the polished floor outside the music room. She ran her duster along the rim of the corridor's wainscotting. The cloth felt soft in her hand. The brown wainscotting lined the walls all the way down the corridor, past Reverend Mother's office, to the staircase in front of the convent's main door.

The corridor was always silent. Even the chattering St. Monica's girls, arriving in their school uniforms for their music lessons, seemed cowed by the brownness, the silence, the polished floor, the high ceiling, as they tiptoed toward the music room without a word. Occasionally a visitor spoke out loud, and a man's laughter or a woman's exclamation echoed down the high long corridor and travelled up the staircase, all the way into the novices' common room on the second floor. Such sounds – hearty "ha-ha-ha"s and a high-pitched, "Well, Sister, I'll be a son of a gun!" – were so weirdly out of place that when they occurred the novices glanced at one another with quizzical looks and laughed silently.

Sister Geraldine had not heard such an outburst since she'd entered the convent nearly two years earlier. She stood still and waited to hear if more sounds might come from the music room. She ran the duster one more time on the wainscotting up and down across from the door. She wondered how long she could keep up the pretence of dusting before someone came out. As she stooped and picked up the mop handle, the figures behind the frosted window appeared closer.

"I told her, 'What I'm required to teach the novices simply isn't sufficient –'" said one voice.

"What did –" said the other.

"I said, 'Surely they should be better prepared. Their young minds should be fed nourishing –'"

"Did she –"

"'It can't be allowed. It is our Rule.' That's all she kept saying. It was like throwing myself against a stone wall, banging my head over and over again."

The voices lowered and the figures moved away from the door. A deep, wordless gasp escaped from the back of Sister Geraldine's throat. Her whole body became taut. The speaker was Mother Alphonsine, the novice mistress. She was, in fact, the superior of the novices, responsible for training them to conform to the Holy Rule of the Order. Mother Alphonsine always appeared placid and in perfect control, strict in her authority, but gentle and kind. She never raised her voice.

Sister Geraldine stood looking at the yellow fringes of the mop. They were dirty and faded with many uses. What was happening? She felt almost disembodied. As if her ears had heard something that the rest of her body, and her mind, did not understand, did not believe, did not want to know.

The door handle was turning, and Sister Geraldine sprang from where she stood and skittered down the corridor toward the back staircase, moving the mop in wild arcs around the floor. The door opened, and she squirmed as she felt someone's eyes on her back. She thought she heard a hesitant intake of breath, as if the novice mistress wondered whether to come after her or not, but then the muffled sound of the habit moved in the opposite direction.

Her sudden action brought her mind back into focus, and Sister Geraldine remembered something that now helped to put the pieces together. On Christmas day, while visiting with her family in one of the parlours, she had seen Mother Alphonsine through the window walking along one of the paths with a young man. The next day at recreation the novice mistress had appeared more animated than usual at recreation.

"My nephew visited me yesterday. He's studying to be a priest. He gave me a book on the Dead Sea Scrolls," she had said, excitement in her voice. Her cheeks were flushed. "These are pieces of parchment that have been found in caves. They were written just before the time of Jesus! Imagine that, and they were found only a few years ago!" With her thumb she smoothed the linen she was embroidering. "I gave the book to Reverend Mother, as of course we're required to do. But I'm sure she'll agree that we should read this book in the novitiate. It will expand our understanding of Holy Scripture."

The novices sat in their usual semicircle facing her, but they were unusually silent in the face of this remark. For Sister Geraldine, the Dead Sea Scrolls seemed a dry and boring topic for recreation.

"When will we be reading it, Mother?" asked a novice finally. She spoke out of politeness, Sister Geraldine thought, in order not to cause the novice mistress embarrassment at the lack of response.

"Well that all depends on Reverend Mother, of course." She continued, encouraged by the novice's question: "My nephew said that they're beginning to learn new things about the Bible now, because the Holy Father has asked scholars to study it more closely. He said that at times we've added things that aren't in the Bible at all. Sentimental things. Like with the Christmas story. There are no oxen or donkeys in St. Luke's account of the birth of Jesus, no –"

A chorus of protests burst forth at this new revelation. "But Mother –"

"No three wise men –"

"Mother . . . !" "What, Mother . . . ?"

"Well, there were wise men, of course, but were there three? We're not told."

"What about gold, frankincense and myrrh, Mother?" Sister Geraldine asked. She felt peevish, as if the ground was slipping beneath her feet and she was desperately trying to hold it in place.

"Well, that's where the number three comes from, of course. But my nephew said that not much is known at all about the early life of Jesus."

"Mother!" "But Mother, it says –" Again, the protests were loud and vehement.

"It's the *meaning* that's important," Mother Alphonsine said. "Nothing will change our faith or our way of life, or our Rule, of course. Nothing changes – it will only deepen our prayer life. Still, if there are things to be learned about Scripture, then of course we must learn them."

Sister Geraldine looked at the faces of the novices around her. Nothing was changing. Their prayer life would only deepen.


BUT – those clandestine whisperings. Mother Alphonsine's words behind the closed door of the music room. Permission had not been given to read that book on the Dead Sea Scrolls. And what was more – the rule of silence was just as important for the nuns as it was for the novices. Not to speak except with permission. Only when necessary. The novice mistress was bound by this rule along with everyone else. In fact, when she spoke to a novice outside of recreation, it was always very brief. With as few words as possible. Only when necessary. Not to do *anything* without permission. And Mother Estelle, the music mistress – had *she* been speaking without permission too?

Near the back staircase, Sister Geraldine passed the piano room where two of the novices were practising a Schubert duet. The two-person striking of the keys, all four hands doing their best to keep up with each other as they drove the music forward, brought some relaxation to her body. A welcome distraction and a reminder of what was to come later.

The pianists were preparing for this evening's concert in honour of the Feast of the Holy Innocents. It was to be the one time in the year when the novices and the nuns' community would have recreation together. "The one time when we can truly appreciate one another's talents," Mother Alphonsine had said with a wink, indicating that there could be a good portion of silliness expected. Indeed, the novices were getting up some of the fun themselves, having started practising a skit during the evening recreation on St. Stephen's Day. The skit involved a young man coming to the door of a crotchety old woman looking for a baby that had just been born. It had the ending that one would expect of a play in which someone looks for a newborn baby at

Christmastime, but there were plenty of hijinks and laughs getting there.

Sister Geraldine climbed slowly up the back staircase, running the mop across each step ahead of her. She desperately wanted not to have heard anything. She felt as though her head had been jerked to the side, and that what might have been glimpsed on the periphery was now being viewed face-on. She had already begun hoping that they would never read this new book. The Gospel descriptions of Jesus's life were vivid and beautiful, and the meditation points that were read every morning from the back of the chapel were just fine. Her novice mistress was tearing apart something that had been carefully put together. She wanted to stay on the narrow path that Mother Alphonsine had set for the novices: the path of the vows and the Holy Rule, the only path of sanctity. She tried to become recollected as she swung the mop rhythmically across the steps in front of her.

This morning's meditation on the Holy Innocents had given much to think about. The points, read aloud as always under the single light bulb, had been more graphic than usual. The reading described with mounting indignation King Herod's jealous rage over the birth of the infant Jesus, and his order that innocent baby boys be killed. "'*See the helpless infants, hear the screeching, the wailing, the whish of the sword as it tears into innocent flesh and slices off tiny heads. Smell the acrid blood, pools of it, as Herod's underlings carry out his diabolical orders. Smell the decaying flesh of these young bodies. Taste the wet, salty tears of the mothers as they try in vain to shield their babes from the soldiers' intent to kill. Prostrate your heart before God now, as He watches with anguish the evil that has been visited upon His beloved people — all in order to kill His Son. He sends an angel to Joseph to take the Holy Child and His blessed mother to Egypt, out of Herod's murderous reach. But must it not grieve God to see the cruelty that the birth of His Son has unleashed so early in His young Life! This is a fulfillment of the prophecy that Rachel is weeping for her children. But in His all-knowing sight, is it not clear to Him that this is but the beginning, that suffering will be the lot of those who follow Him? Let us bow before these tiny, helpless children, the first martyrs for the faith . . .* '" One baby after another, senselessly killed. The reading had sobered Sister Geraldine, casting a shadow over the generally joyous Christmas meditations. But now, the image of the dead babies and their sobbing mothers matched her own sombre, disconnected emotions.

Sister Geraldine knew nothing about Mother Alphonsine. The novice mistress's face was naturally pale, even yellowish, and when she smiled, lines crinkled at the sides of her eyes, and her mouth opened wide, revealing broad teeth and the flash of gold somewhere in the back. Her smile appeared only at recreation. At most other times, she remained straight-faced and serious. She had reprimanded Sister Geraldine on many occasions, as she had the other novices. If a novice broke the rule of silence, or wasted food, or acted against obedience, she instructed the novice to make reparation: to kneel before the other novices and accuse herself of the failing. But this was only fair and right. She kept the Holy Rule and was training the novices to do the same. She was their superior and every word she spoke came to them as the will of God. But now ...

"This is our last recreation before the new year, Mother," said one of the novices during the afternoon recreation a few hours later.

"That's right." Mother Alphonsine looked up and spoke with surprise, as if she hadn't realized what date it was. As if she was relieved to have something to say, something to take her mind off other things. Her smile seemed forced, and she pulled hard on her blue embroidery thread, almost allowing the linen in her hand to pucker. Her needlework was usually done with much more ease. Her eyes looked tired and vulnerable.

"That's right," the novice mistress said again with forced enthusiasm. "There's the concert tonight and then the three-day silent retreat, and then –" She looked around at the group of novices sitting side by side in a semicircle facing her. "Then it will be not only a new year but a new *decade!*" She smiled more widely than usual, and her teeth looked dull and yellow.

"Nineteen sixty, Mother," a few of the novices said in unison.

"That's right." Again the forced smile, the lines around her eyes. "Nineteen sixty."

"The Fatima secret will be revealed in 1960," said Sister Lucy.

"Oh, Mother, yes." There was a gaggle of choruses. "Mother, do you think –" "Will the Holy Father –" "I wonder what the secret is!"

"Has the bishop said anything, Mother?" asked Sister Lucy. She was petite, with a timid, peaked face, but sat tall and straight in her chair.

"What on earth would the bishop have to say?" Mother Alphonsine's voice was suddenly sharp, and Sister Geraldine felt around her a collective gasp. She left her own needle stuck halfway into the stocking she was darning, and felt that others had stopped their sewing as well.

There was silence until Sister Lucy spoke again, in a tiny, scared voice. "I thought he might know when the secret is going to be revealed. The secret that Our Lady told at Fatima."

"The bishop has more important things to do." Mother Alphonsine kept her eyes on her cloth and again pulled her thread tight. Her voice seemed to have gained a measure of equilibrium again, and the novices' hands, one by one, began once again to run their needles in and out of their various cloths. "The Lourdes secret is in the hands of the Holy Father, and only he will decide when, or if, to reveal it. Everything is in the hands of God."

"That reminds me of a story I heard once," said a novice at the far end of the semicircle. "A ship was in a storm at sea and rocking back and forth, and a woman passenger came up to the captain and asked if they were in any danger of the ship sinking. The captain said, 'We're in God's hands,

Madam,' and the woman said, 'Oh, is it as bad as that?'"

She stopped and looked around. No one else spoke. The novice continued, blushing at the lack of response, "A priest told us that story at a school retreat, Mother. The idea is that we're always in God's hands no matter what, and the woman thought that things were in God's hands only when there was no other way out."

"We're *always* in God's hands, but God helps those who help themselves." Again, the novice mistress's voice sounded unusually impatient.

Heads remained bowed and needles ran up and down through cloth. Scissors snipped and the pieces of fabric around the circle rustled lightly. Sister Geraldine ran her darning needle back and forth, cut the yarn and reached into her bag for another black skein, licked the end of the thread and passed it through the needle's eye. She had never been so grateful for a half-darned hole. Her wrist moved rhythmically as she wove the point of her needle across the taut black lines, working up, over and down the weave. Woof crossing warp. Up, over and down and under. Up, over and down and under, like the captain's ship casting on the waves. *We're in God's hands, Madam.*

Finally, a brave novice spoke in a shaky voice. "Mother, are we going to practise our skit?"

"We shouldn't take time from our needlework, should we, Mother?" said another.

Mother Alphonsine rubbed her lips together and sat even more upright than usual. She ran her needle through her linen and let her hands rest upon its folds. "Yes, we will take time from our needlework. This one time. In honour of the Holy Innocents. Put your sewing away and make some space here in front." She folded her cloth and smiled with, Sister Geraldine thought, a hint of defiance.

The novices whooped with choruses of "Mother!" "Yes, Mother!" They grinned at one another, and even pasty little Sister Lucy's smile lit up her face as they stood up and jostled silently together to put their black bags away in the back cupboard and shunted the chairs aside.

No one, Sister Geraldine noticed, had asked further about the book Mother Alphonsine had talked about so enthusiastically two days earlier. Were the other novices as uncertain as she was about wanting to learn new and unwanted things about the Bible? Well, Reverend Mother wasn't allowing it. That was settled. Yet Mother Alphonsine. . . .


THE OUTER DOOR to the sacristy was closed when Sister Geraldine arrived later in the afternoon to set up for the next day's Mass. She stopped still and gaped. The door was never closed except for confessions, the priest using the sacristy as his side of the confessional, sitting in his chair, and the nuns kneeling before the wooden grate in the tiny anteroom between the sacristy and the main corridor leading to the chapel. This was not confession day. There would be a chance for confessions only on the last day of the year, the last day of the Christmas retreat. What was happening here, and how was she going to be able to set up for Mass?

She looked around. The voice behind the door sounded agitated, even angry. Should she go and find Mother Alphonsine? How were the vestments going to be laid out if she couldn't get into the sacristy? Could she go in the sacristy if the priest was in there hearing someone's confession? No, it wasn't possible. Where was Mother Alphonsine? She caught her breath and tiptoed closer to the door, straining to hear. No, it was a sin to hear another's confession deliberately.

She moved back and entered the chapel, uncertain of what to do next. Ahead, the sanctuary was alive in Christmas resplendence. The crèche had been set up by one of the nuns just inside the communion rail. Brown paper had been expertly crushed and marked with pastel crayons, and it looked for all the world like a cave. Inside, of course, stood all the Christmas figures, except for the star and the wise men, which sat on the sacristy table, ready to be added on the vigil of the Epiphany. The *three* wise men. The scene was festooned with poinsettia plants and a Christmas tree. The pine fragrance filled the chapel.

In front of Our Lady's and St. Joseph's altars were the baskets and arrangements of flowers sent by families of the nuns. Her own family's was a modest arrangement of small white chrysanthemums and red carnations. It looked rather puny beside the baskets of large mums and roses and the huge banks of poisettias, but she knew her mother would have agonized over a choice of flowers that would last a long time and wouldn't cost much. On the high altar the brass pots of Boston ferns gleamed in the late afternoon light and the gold tabernacle curtain stood like a sentinel to the Holy of Holies. The door leading from the sanctuary to the sacristy was closed as always whenever there were confessions.

She turned to see Mother Estelle beckoning to her from the chapel door. The nun pointed upward with one finger and blinked at her behind round, thick glasses. Sister Geraldine stared. "Upstairs," Mother Estelle whispered.

"Mother, I have to –" she began, pointing to the closed sacristy door. "What's happening, Mother?"

Mother Estelle glanced around. "Anyone may ask for an extraordinary confessor at any time. Our Holy Rule allows it. It's nobody's business." She spoke in a whisper that was barely audible. She continued pointing upward, blinking and stern, and then turned abruptly and left the chapel.

Sister Geraldine closed her eyes. She wanted desperately to hold onto something. She hated the unsureness of all that seemed to be happening around her. Mother Estelle had told her to go upstairs, but Mother Estelle wasn't her superior, was she? She walked up the side aisle, to Our Lady's altar, toward her family's flower arrangement. Shiny balls and clusters of pine cones were nestled in among the blossoms. She imagined her mother, who loved baubles of any kind, picking out the colourful balls with the thought that this Christmasy addition would bring a sparkle to her daughter's eye and remind her of home. She ran her finger around the edge of the container and bent over, breathing in the scent of the bouquet.

The sacristy door opened and a priest stepped out, tall and lanky, and his soutane swished down the aisle and out the chapel door. Sister Geraldine saw a nun appear from somewhere to usher him down the corridor. The sacristy was now free. Inside, she saw immediately that the door at the far end, the one with the confessional grille, was still closed. She hurried over to open it, and then stood still. There were voices on the other side.

"I told him I'm not being allowed –" Mother Alphonsine was saying.

Mother Estelle's voice murmured something that Sister Geraldine couldn't hear.

"He laughed." Mother Alphonsine's voice sounded resigned, defeated.

"He laughed?" said Mother Estelle.

"He said, 'Well, what can I do?' He has no authority to do anything."

The voices lowered and moved away. Slowly, Sister Geraldine opened the narrow door where the chasubles hung in their various colours. Liturgical colours. It wasn't so long ago that she had been ignorant of which liturgical colours were to be used on which occasions, but now it felt as if she had known about them forever. She pulled out the red chasuble. Red for martyrs. Two martyrs' feast days in a row this Christmas week. She took the chasuble from its hanger and laid it out: the first vestment to be placed on the Mass table, the last that the priest would pull over his head the next morning.

For the past two years she had been trying to conform herself to the will of God by learning to be a good nun, to follow Mother Alphonsine's teaching on the vows. And surely that was the right thing to do. She would continue to do that, certainly she would. Look at all the intelligent, holy women living in the community, those who had taught her at St. Monica's — they were all living with the serene knowledge that they were fulfilling God's will, that they held the secret of a holy Christian life. The secret — that was it — the secret of the way of life that Christ desired: to follow the will of the superior in every respect. It was the only path to holiness; Mother Alphonsine had said that many times. And now Mother Alphonsine herself was really only trying to do what was best for the novices, wasn't she? Trying to follow the will of God?

THAT EVENING, the black-veiled nuns filed into the auditorium where the novices had set up chairs. All stood aside as Reverend Mother came forward, her face leathery and wrinkled. She walked straight to the chair in the centre that had wooden arms and a black cushion on the seat. The nuns gathered around her wearing smiles. There was a general movement of shuffling chairs and black serge and rosary beads as they all found seats. Mother Alphonsine was nowhere to be seen. Mother Estelle had presided at supper in the novices' refectory and, when the after-supper chores were over, had ushered them into the room for the concert.

The skit began. The novice playing the man swaggered onto the stage with her veil tied behind her back, a thin moustache painted on her face and a rough jacket covering the top part of her habit. The nuns laughed and clapped, and one of them exclaimed, "Mother, isn't it wonderful how much can be done with so little!" Reverend Mother let a flicker of a smile pass over her face as the skit ended. Then three nuns with large red polka-dot bows pinned to their wimples did a tap dance. The audience clapped and cheered and one of the nuns said, "Oh, wouldn't the girls at St. Monica's love to see this, Mother!" The two novices who were to play the duet moved into position on the piano bench, and afterwards again there was clapping and exclamations of "Oh that's beautiful!" Then all the novices stood up, smiling and gesturing as to where they should place themselves so that those singing each of the three parts could stand together. Mother Estelle sat at the piano and played the introduction to "How Lovely Is Thy Dwelling Place" and with an exaggerated nod of her head as their cue, they began to sing.

When they finished, the nuns clapped and cheered. "Oh, Mother, the loveliness of young voices!" said one. Reverend Mother stood up and the nuns followed suit. "Thanks to all for the beautiful concert," she said. "And may we all have a fruitful three-day retreat. Praise be to Jesus."

"Amen," everyone murmured, and made the sign of the cross. Reverend Mother turned and walked toward the back door and the nuns, some carrying chairs to the side of the room, followed in silence. The novices filed out behind the departing nuns, the whole group, white veils after black, looking like an outsized magpie. Sister Geraldine stood in the shadow of the stage folding the discarded costumes of the skit and watched Mother Estelle as she put down the lid of the piano and collected the music sheets. The nun went over then to check the windows, reaching up to make sure each one was locked. Sister Geraldine approached her.

"Mother."

Mother Estelle gasped and turned, and then put her finger to her mouth. Her eyes, through round thick glasses, were wide with questioning and disapproval.

"Mother, is something wrong with Mother Alphonsine? Is she sick?"

"This is the Great Silence, child. Go up to bed this minute." The words came out in a hissing whisper. Mother Estelle moved to the next window and reached up to the lock.

"There's something wrong, isn't there, Mother?"

She turned again toward Sister Geraldine. "This is very wrong of *you*. *Go – to – bed!*"

Sister Geraldine kept in step with her as she moved to the next window. "Mother Alphonsine wanted us to read a book that she got for Christmas, something about the Dead Sea. Reverend Mother said no." She was uncertain of what to say next.

Mother Estelle whirled around and stared at her. "How do you know this?" Her voice was sharp.

"She told us at recreation. She thought Reverend Mother would say yes." She hesitated. "But I know that Reverend Mother said no. Why, Mother?"

Mother Estelle glanced toward the door, then spoke, this time in a half-whisper. "Mother Alphonsine has a very responsible role, training you young people to be good religious. She wants you to have the opportunity to learn new things about Scripture. But if Reverend Mother says no, we don't ask why. 'Why' has no place in religious obedience."

"I didn't want to read that stuff anyway, Mother, but I just wonder –"

"It is not 'that stuff.' And it's not for you or anyone to say what you want or don't want. Do you not know this by now? Do you not know that you take what is given you without question? What *you* want makes no difference at all. Sometimes we all have to be reminded of these things, even a novice mistress. Otherwise, who knows what would happen if we all got ideas of our own?"

"Mother . . ." Sister Geraldine paused, not knowing what to say. She wanted Mother Estelle to tell her that everything was firm and clear in the novitiate, as it had always been. In God's hands. "Mother, where's Mother Alphonsine? Why wasn't she here tonight?"

The nun turned sharply and stared again at Sister Geraldine, then turned back and continued to the door, reaching for the light switches. One by one she shut them until the pair could see each other only by the light of the corridor. Her face was now in shadow. "We've committed a sin by speaking unnecessarily during the Great Silence. It's only a venial sin, of course, but still it should be mentioned in confession." She hesitated a moment, considering what to say next. "Anything said in confession need not be reported to the superior. It says this in our Holy Rule." She hesitated again. "At least, it's there somewhere in our Holy Rule. I'm pretty sure it is." She led the way down the corridor and waited for Sister Geraldine to reach the back staircase. Then she turned out the corridor light and the two climbed the staircase in the dark.

MOTHER ESTELLE sat in the chair behind the novice mistress's desk. The three-day retreat had passed in total silence, the novices doing their usual chores: the kitchen wash-up, the clearing of the refectory, the vegetable peeling, the mopping and dusting. Sister Geraldine kept on with her sacristan's duties, laying out the priest's vestments and readying the sanctuary for morning Mass each day, and clearing things away afterward. Every afternoon, the novices pulled on their rubber overshoes, drew their woollen shawls about their shoulders and took their usual half-hour walk around the convent grounds – along the frozen riverbank, behind the laundry extension, on the sidewalk to Our Lady's grotto and back along the side of the chapel. At moments when they passed one another, they exchanged glances, quizzical, furtive.

Then they bowed to each other and moved on. Passing Sister Lucy one day, Sister Geraldine thought at first that the other novice was going to speak. She stopped and looked directly at Sister Geraldine, her cheeks red and her breath white and wispy from the cold. Then she too bowed her head, pulled her shawl tightly around her and moved past.

The novices now sat opposite Mother Estelle in their semicircle, their hands folded on their laps. They were dressed in their Sunday veils and habits, all a bit stiffer than their everyday clothing. Needlework was nowhere in sight, the first day of January being the octave of Christmas and a holy day of obligation, and therefore treated like a Sunday, when no work except the most necessary was to be done.

"Mother Alphonsine has not been well and has had to go away for a rest. You will be getting a new novice mistress. She will be arriving later today from one of our other houses. Reverend Mother has asked me to take recreation with you this afternoon." Mother Estelle clasped and unclasped her hands as she spoke. Her eyes, behind thick glasses, passed back and forth across the top of the room. "And so now, after three days of silence – Praise be to Jesus!" Her face brightened and she smiled at the semicircle of white veiled heads facing her. "It's 1960! Happy New Year!"

## *Acknowledgements*

Earlier versions of some of the stories in this collection were previously published in *The Antigonish Review, The Dalhousie Review,* and *paperbytes.* Grateful acknowledgement is made to the Canada Council for the Arts, the Ontario Arts Council and the Toronto Arts Council. Warm thanks to Cynthia Holz and to my writing group, especially Barry Webster. And a big debt of gratitude to the Banff Centre for the Arts, to Coteau Books and, in particular, to Edna Alford.

## *About the Author*

MARY FRANCES COADY's short fiction has been published in several literary journals. She has also written biographies and a young adult novel. As well, she has given writing workshops at various venues in the Toronto area. Born in Saskatchewan and raised in Alberta, she has worked as a teacher, an editor, and a journalist. She now lives in Toronto, where she works as a sessional university instructor.

## ENVIRONMENTAL BENEFITS STATEMENT

**Coteau Books** saved the following resources by printing the pages of this book on chlorine free paper made with 100% post-consumer waste.

| TREES | WATER | SOLID WASTE | GREENHOUSE GASES |
|---|---|---|---|
| **7** | **3,376** | **205** | **701** |
| FULLY GROWN | GALLONS | POUNDS | POUNDS |

Calculations based on research by Environmental Defense and the Paper Task Force.
Manufactured at Friesens Corporation